Also by Tyler Cook

A Guide to Historic Dillsboro

The One

Tyler Cook

Moonshine Press • Franklin, North Carolina

Though the premise of this novel was inspired by an actual event, this is a work of fiction. Names, characters, places, and incidents are either the product of the author's imagination or are used fictitiously. Any resemblance to any actual persons, living or dead, or to any place or event, is coincidental.

Published by:
Moonshine Press
162 Riverwood Drive
Franklin, NC 28734

www.moonshinepressnc.com

International Standard Book Number : 978-1505458046

Thank you to Henry Fichner for providing this wonderful cover. Thanks to Chris Dobson and Caitlyn Parker for being one of the first people to read the book and provide reviews. And most importantly, thank you to all of my family and friends for supporting me through this incredible journey, even though they had no idea what the book was about. I love you all!

This book is dedicated to my great-aunt,
Eva McCall,
my fellow author, my friend, my inspiration.

"In this world, if it's the only thing I've ever learnt, is that everything you love can hurt. And the only thing you are is a child of the universe." — Delta Goodrem

Prologue

Late Summer of 2009

Eli Cooper walked into math class a few minutes before the bell would ring. He had a stitch in his chest from walking so fast from the end of the building to where he was now. Eli always liked getting to each class early and preparing for the period ahead of him. He thought it showed his willingness to learn and to get the grade he deserved. For some, they would have called it "kissing ass."

At sixteen, with a very thin body and a face full of pepperoni pimples, Eli didn't have the luxury of a social life. It wasn't like he was unpopular; he had friends in school. But it took a while for Eli to warm up to people. Under the thin layer of skin that covered up his bony structure, lied a pool full of personality.

As time passed, more people started to follow suit and walked into the classroom, wanting to talk to friends in class more than preparing for the lesson ahead. Conversations began to buzz around the room, turning a once quiet area into a roaring space as students began taking their seats.

Eli bent over to grab his textbook out of his bag. It had been only two weeks since Eli returned to Pinecrest High School to start his junior year. So far, things were going great for him, for the most part. He had adjusted to his new schedule, learned the names of his teachers, and began making a few friends in each class.

He began observing the conversations around him, waiting for someone to come up and start a conversation with him, or to be invited into an ongoing discussion. So far, though, nothing. His acquaintance, Allie Gordon, which he usually spoke to, was not there yet.

Out of the blue, he saw his best friend, Tori, quickly waving to him as she was walking to her class. She was a petite young girl, with blonde hair below her shoulders and skin as light as Casper the ghost. She was a year younger than Eli, but more mature than some of the children Eli's age. Eli tried to wave back at her, but she was gone before he could lift his hand.

The bell rang, which prompted Eli to move his eyes from the classroom door, which had been looking for Allie, towards the teacher, who would begin to call roll and start the class. When Mrs. Roper bent down to read the names off the attendance sheet, her red hair fell to the sides of her face, preventing her from seeing anyone entering the room.

Fortunately for Allie, Mrs. Roper didn't see her as she slid into the room undetected.

Allie wiped her forehead with relief as she made her way to the back of the room, where a seat behind Eli was reserved.

"Close call," Eli muttered, his head turned towards Allie, mocking her common lateness. Why Eli wasn't used to it by now, he didn't know.

Allie tried to squeeze into the seat of her chair, which was quite uncomfortable for her because of her obese weight. She was a pretty girl though, with designer glasses, a light layer of makeup on her face, and straight, blonde hair that was tied up in a ponytail.

"Sorry," she whispered. She didn't want Mrs. Roper to give any reason to suspect that she was late.

"Eli Cooper," Mrs. Roper called out, her head lifting up to look in Eli's direction.

"Here," he said, raising his hand and turning around to make eye contact with his teacher. He returned the smile that she gave him and turned his body around so he was again facing the front of the room.

Eli and Allie continued to talk in hushed tones throughout the rest of the roll call. Allie was talking about how she never had a boyfriend, while her brother was getting dates left and right from all of the girls in the school. And of course, she expected Eli to listen to every word of it and give her advice that would help—

"Sorry I'm late." Someone busted through the door, not only making a noise by talking, but by slamming the door shut by accident as they entered.

All eyes were on the intruder of the room, some startled by the slamming door that abruptly cut off their little conversations. Even Eli turned around to see the source of the noise.

"Mr. Lance," an irritable Mrs. Roper gasped, her left hand clutched to her chest as the pencil in her right hand continued to stay on the roll call paper. Once the initial shock faded away, she said, "Thank you for joining us. Had I had known that you would be making such an entrance, I would have suggested that you stay outside."

Christian Lance, a tall, stocky boy at the age of eighteen, stood at the front of the room with all eyes on him. His backpack was hanging off of his back, with one strap over his shoulder. Afraid to move to his seat, he clutched the strap to ensure that the bag wouldn't fall out on the floor for the whole class to see. Carefully, trying to not bring more attention on himself than could already be possible, he said, "Sorry, but I—"

"Please, Mr. Lance, spare me. If you have enough energy to make an excuse, you have enough energy to make it here on time. Now, if I recall correctly," she looked down at her watch and tapped it, "It has been 30 seconds since I called your name. Which makes you late. If you will please, sit down so we are no longer wasting the class' time."

Wow, Eli thought. *Usually, I enjoy her, or any teacher for that matter, getting onto students for being late. But this is just harsh.*

When Christian realized that his teacher was finished with him, he turned and started heading to his seat. Waves of sniggers and giggles flooded the room. The students that usually sat around him didn't hold back and laughed as he sat down.

Right next to Eli.

"Now that Mr. Lance has had his moment in the spotlight for today, we shall begin," said Mrs. Roper, heading to the podium with a textbook in hand.

While the students were turning their textbooks to the page that their teacher instructed them, Eli looked at Christian.

A little heavy-set, Christian could be seen taking deep breaths to try and calm himself. Clearly, he was embarrassed, if not humiliated, his face burning red and sweaty. Eli looked at his hair, noticing the silver patches that were beginning to overtake the black hair that Christian had.

This event will surely add more grey, Eli thought to himself. *Poor guy, do boys this young get gray hair?*

The boy in front of Christian turned around and looked at

him, a grin from ear to ear.

Eli knew the boy well, or knew *of* the boy well. Barry Grant was in the same year as Eli. A well known member of the 2010 class, Barry used his good looks, and his fists, to get what he wanted. Eli had heard rumors that he would humiliate, if not beat up any guy that appeared vulnerable or different from himself, no matter their age.

But no matter how mean Barry acted towards others, how disgusting he looked after degrading someone that he just finished humiliating, Eli couldn't help thinking how cute he was—

Cute? Did Eli really just think of another guy as cute?

Why do I have to think that way about the biggest creep in the school?

"Hey, Lance," Barry said, his smile now a smirk, a clear indication that he was about to work his demon magic. "Could you have put on a better show? What'll you do next? Come in dancing like the fairy you are?"

Barry's friends erupted in laughter which was so loud, that it attracted the attention of Mrs. Roper, who began lecturing them for causing a second interruption in her classroom that day.

They quieted up after Mrs. Roper's lecture, but the gang still snickered and made faces in Christian's direction throughout the entire class period.

Eli tried not to look at Christian; another set a eyes that he knew Christian didn't want looking at him. But he couldn't help taking a quick look at him and notice one big teardrop make its way down Christian's face.

***

Several days passed, and there was no sign of Christian at

school or in class.

Eli made a promise that if Christian ever did come back to school, that he would go to him and apologize for the way he was treated, even though he was not at fault for the horrible episode that took place in math class. He knew that Christian needed a friend, and he was going to be there for him, no matter what anybody, especially his crush, Barry, thought about him.

***

On Friday, Eli made his way to math like the many days before. Except this time, he managed to have Tori tag along with him. They stopped in front of Mrs. Roper's class, Eli waiting beside the door to finish his conversation with his friend.

"Come on, Eli, you know that you wanna go see *New Moon* with me! I need to see my Edward again!" Tori stood there with a contemplating look on her face. "However," she said, "It wouldn't be too bad to see Jacob either."

She slapped him on the arm when he didn't respond. "Stop keeping me hanging, and say that you will go!"

As Eli was still making up his mind on whether to go the movie with Tori, and risk getting excited by looking at Taylor Lautner in front of other people, he looked inside the classroom, which immediately stopped his thinking process.

"Hello?" Tori shoved Eli slightly toward the wall to get his attention back. "Are you even paying attention to me?"

He's back, thought Eli.

There he stood. Christian Lance was back in class. Eli knew that the event with coming into the class late would cause Christian to come a little bit earlier, but not earlier than Eli.

"Hold on, Tori," Eli finally said as she kept poking him to get his attention. "One of my classmates is back."

He observed both Christian and Mrs. Roper bent over what appeared to be a pink sheet of paper. Christian's hair seemed to have more gray in it than the last time Eli saw him. He couldn't hear what they were saying, nor could he read what was on the paper from such a far distance. After talking between them for a little bit longer, Mrs. Roper reached out for a pen on her desk, and signed her name at the bottom. She handed it back to Christian and walked away.

Eli shushed Tori as Christian started walking towards the door. This was his chance.

"Hi, Christian, I—"

Christian ran into Eli, causing Eli to jump out of his way. Either Christian had no idea that Eli had spoken to him, or he thought Eli was just as bad as the rest of the class.

Eli and Tori both looked at Christian walking away.

"What a douche," said Tori. "What the hell was his problem?"

Eli didn't answer. All he could do was watch Christian walk out of the school, realizing he missed a chance at being a friend to someone who needed it.

Part One
Six Years Later

Chapter One

Early 2014

Eli shook his head, indicating his resistance to the idea. "No way, Tori."

"Oh come on Eli, live a little!"

They both sat in Tori's small office that was located in the back of *Arcade Hut*, where they both worked. *Arcade Hut* was an arcade center that filled up an old dance studio that closed down decades ago. In its prime, the place was the central location for entertainment of all ages. Since then, it became the place for young children and rebellious teenagers. Eli was hired there a year prior to his high school graduation. With his help, Tori managed to also become an employee six months following his hiring.

As the years passed, Eli and Tori eventually became the oldest employees on the payroll. But, while Tori climbed the *Hut's* small ladder of heirarchy, Eli continually declined the offers to be promoted and instead pursued his college education. Tori's job was to tend to the paperwork and billing, while taking a few college classes on the side.

Working together had only strengthened the bond that Eli and Tori had together. They always had something to talk about, even if it resorted to gossiping about anything and anyone that came to mind.

Tori pointed at her computer again. "This is your last chance for happiness."

Eli laughed, trying to dodge the awkward conversation that

was taking place. "You don't know that."

"Yes I do," she said. "You have spent years looking for someone, and haven't found anybody worth anything. How are you supposed to find a guy if you don't start broadening your horizons?"

Here she goes again.

It had been a year since Eli confided in Tori that he was attracted to both sexes. At the time, he thought he would go crazy if someone didn't know of his secret. The thought of having someone else share his burden made it feel less heavy on himself. Tori took the news better than expected, but now thought it was her job to set him up with every guy that seemed to swing on the same team. He had put up with her persistence to find someone because she had accepted his secret, but now she was starting to bug him about the issue.

"You know I have met people. They just weren't the right people for me."

"You're too picky. I don't know how you're gonna find a gay guy that has decided to wait for the 'right person'. If you find someone like that in Forrester County, you need to grab him and marry him!"

They both laughed at her comment. Sure she could be a pain, but Eli loved her. And he knew she only wanted to make him happy.

Tori got up, and rolled Eli's chair around her desk so they could both view the computer.

"Now," she said, "A lot of people join POF to meet people." She started loading a page on her browser. "There is no shame in doing this."

"POF?" Eli had a confused look on his face. "What the hell is POF?"

"Duh," Tori replied cynically, obviously surprised that Eli hadn't had already done his research. "It means Plenty of Fish. You know the saying: "There is plenty of fish in the sea.""

"Okay, I get it now," Eli said. "Hopefully there is a fish in this internet pond of yours for me."

"Sure there will," she said hopefully.

After several minutes of making the account, Tori informed Eli that they now needed to start filling out the specifics of himself.

"Okay...," Eli started. He didn't know what to say about himself, let alone something that would be appealing to other people.

"Let's start simple," Tori then said, knowing that Eli was going to make the thing a bigger deal than it was supposed to be. "Here we go. How would you describe your body type?"

Eli looked down and observed his own physique.

In the years since high school, Eli had grown to be an attractive, young man. With the help of his father, Charlie, Eli was able to build his muscles, as well as his weight. The eyesores on his face had been removed and now showed clear skin. But his hair remained the same, short and spiky. The way Eli always liked it.

"Toned, I guess," he said, unsure of himself.

"Agreed. Okay, do you have children?"

Eli looked at Tori like she was now the dumb one.

"Oh yeah," she said. "My bad."

After several more minutes of interrogating Eli, she was able to form a nearly complete profile of him. Now all she needed was no more thing...

"NO!"

"Why not," She questioned, "How is the love of your live supposed to meet you, if you don't give a picture to show what you look like?"

"It's called discretion, Tori. If I wanted the whole world to know my sexual preferences, I would have done so already." Eli was finally ready to stand his ground. "No, no picture."

Tori rolled her eyes. *It is 2014, Eli,* she thought. *When are you going to stop hiding who you really are?* "Okay," she said, "No picture."

And it was done. They both looked over it several times to make sure they hadn't missed any details, or made sure that what was on his profile looked appealing to the people on the other screen.

"It's as good as it's gonna get," Eli said.

No one ever finds the love of their life on these things.

"It could use a little more flare, but for a beginner, it looks pretty good," said Tori.

"Yeah," he replied, mocking her, "I'm so glad I came to the Forrester County matchmaker for this."

Tori pointed a finger at him. "Don't give me any bull. Don't forget, I outrank you now at work. And I can have you fired anytime I want to."

Eli knew she was only kidding, but decided to play along with her. He started acting like a little scared child and started running in circles!

"Oh no! A secretary! Please don't bring your wrath down on me!"

"Office Assistant! Get it right!"

19

Eli was all serious now. "If you keep focusing more on this place than on your education, that's exactly where you'll stay!"

"Get outta here," she said, waving him out of the room. She knew he had a point. "You better get out there. If you go over on your break, Marie will be on my ass."

"Don't let her bust your balls too much," Eli responded.

They both laughed.

***

When Eli made it home later that night, he was exhausted. Pulling into the driveway of his home couldn't have been any sweeter.

I can't wait to get a clean shower and go to bed.

He put his Civic Hybrid in park, and made his way into the house.

The house was silent, which was surprising to Eli. Any other time of the day, there would be some sort of commotion going on in there.

Eli decided not to question it for too long, and decided to savor it after a long day of loud games, screaming kids, and bitchy parents.

He went into his parents' bedroom, like he did every night when he worked late. Even though he knew they were in a deep sleep, and they wouldn't remember him even saying that he had returned home, he knew that he would get a lecture if they found out that he hadn't reported in.

"Night," he said in a normal tone. He didn't bother lowering his voice. They were both out of it.

"Huh," his mom, Diane, and dad grunted.

Pleased with the response that he got, he decided to go

upstairs.

Located on the third floor of his family's rather large house, was Eli's room. Eli leaned toward his sisters' rooms to catch any indication that his sisters were up. When he didn't hear anything, he went on into his room, and shut the door.

He had just removed his shoes from his aching feet when he heard his phone buzzing. He knew before he read the message who it was from.

It was from Tori.

Don't forget to check POF!!! Find the man of your dreams! *Yeah, good luck with that.*

He tossed the phone onto his bed and turned around and turned on his computer.

"Might as well humor her," he said to himself.

After several long minutes of waiting on his computer to load, his browser finally brought up POF. Tori had spent so much time decorating his profile that she had forgotten to show him what to do.

What now?

He started clicking around to see what was there for him. Half of the time, the site asked him to upgrade to their premium service. Other times, he came across profiles of people that he knew of, and wouldn't touch them with a ten-foot poll.

After about thirty minutes of browsing the site, and not seeing anything promising, he grabbed his phone off the bed and started texting Tori.

This is such a waste of time. I already know these creeps on here.

A couple of seconds later, a buzz indicated Tori's response.

How about you filter the profiles. Narrow your search.

Whatever you say.

So instead of searching for profiles with pictures and people 20 miles around him, he decided to narrow his search by selecting the profiles that didn't have a face picture, and were located closer to him. He clicked for the new search results.

One profile appeared.

Curious of the one person that fit the strong filters that he put in place, Eli clicked on the profile.

Eli liked what he saw.

Hi there! I am techgeek4. I am currently a college student pursuing computer technology at *Pinecrest University.* **I love the outdoors, which includes hiking or anything else in that category. I am an avid reader, while also enjoying TV and music. My journey here has a long story behind it, so I won't bore you with the details. In a nutshell, I'm looking for friends, and hopefully in the future, something more. If this meets your criteria, don't hesitate to send me a message!**

Perfect!

After the initial excitement, Eli tried to calm himself down.

Chances are that he'll stop talking as soon as he knows who you are, or sees a picture of you.

But it didn't hurt to find out what this guy had to offer. Maybe he could be *the one.*

Eli looked down towards the top of the profile. In the corner, there was a green light that had ONLINE next to it.

Eli couldn't resist the temptation. He had to message him.

Hi.

Eli immediately regretted the one-worded message.

Wow, what a way to show personality there, buddy!

Just when he got his hopes up, there was ding.

Eli looked closely to see a response from techgeek4. He clicked.

Hello there, sir.

I'm glad I haven't already screwed that up.

How are you today?

Ding.

I'm great and yourself?

I'm great, thanks. Eli started to click SEND when he paused. Maybe it was time to find out who this guy was. He resumed typing. **I noticed that your profile says that you're currently in Pinecrest, NC. Have you recently moved into the area?**

Ding.

No, I've lived here all my live. All 24 years.

He's only 2 years older than me!

Eli started figuring it up, and realized that this guy would have been at Pinecrest High School at the same time as he was.

With any luck, I'll know him.

I've lived here all my life too. Say, it is very possible that we went to the same school together. You went to Pinecrest High School, right?

Ding.

For a few years. I left to go somewhere else on my last year.

Eli kept typing.

Okay, but that would mean that there was still a chance that we saw each other. Maybe even knew each other. What's

your name?

Techgeek4 replied. **I don't wanna say. I'm not out.**

I coulda seen that coming. He wants me to tell him my name, and when he realizes I'm not his type, he'll ditch the conversation.

Listen, I'm not out either. So if you're worried that I'll blab your secret all over town, don't be. Your secret is safe with me. I'll tell you my name first, if that makes you feel better.

What are you doing? He thought to himself. *You're going to out yourself to someone who may know you and may expose you!*

Ding.

Okay that sounds fair.

Okay, if you want to possibly find love, it'll be a chance you'll have to take.

Okay, I'm Eli Cooper. What about you?

No response.

Well, another one bites the dust.

He sat there for a couple of minutes, and no response was given. It had become evident to Eli that this guy wasn't going to respond to him.

Eli got out of his seat and made his way to his closet to gather clothes for his shower. He was walking into his bathroom when he heard a ding.

Eli dropped his clothes on the bathroom counter and ran back into his room to read the message. *Please Lord, please let him be* the one.

Okay…I'm Christian Lance.

Chapter Two

"You have got to be kidding me," Eli said out loud.

Could this be the same guy that I think he is? No, he left years ago…

Knowing if this was the same guy that was in his math class was killing Eli. He had to know if this was the same guy.

Say, Eli typed, **that name sounds familiar. Did you happen to be in Mrs. Roper's math class once upon a time?**

Ding.

I was. For a couple of weeks. Your name sounds familiar too, but I can't seem to put a name with a face.

So it is him, thought Eli.

I believe we were in the same class.

Ding.

Could you happen to send me a picture of you? That way I can remember who I am talking to, ha-ha.

He already knows my name, so there isn't any more harm in showing him my face.

Eli typed his agreement and started searching for a picture of himself that would represent him in the best way. Finally, after a few moments of going through his photo collection, he chose one. The same one that Tori had wanted to set as his profile picture. He clicked SEND.

Ah, yes. I remember you now.

Can I get one of you as well? It has been so long since I

have seen you.

> **Sure, hold on.**

Eli sat there and waiting for him to reciprocate. But nothing. *Wow, Eli, you have already run him off. Are you really that scary looking?*

Ding.

Eli clicked open the picture, and was shocked by what he saw.

The picture before him was not of the same Christian Lance that he knew years ago. Yes, many features in his face remained the same. But for the most part, the man was so different to Eli. The once stocky boy was now lean, and from what Eli could tell from the picture, even muscular. His face was no longer full. And the messy, gray-patched hair had been replaced by black, spiked hair.

Damn, Eli thought. *Time has been well to you, Mr. Lance.*

He started typing his response. He was already regretting what he was doing, but he couldn't help himself.

> **Yes, I remember you clearly now. You are WAY cuter than I remember you, though.**

> **Ha-ha. Thank you. You look pretty good yourself.**

> **Thank you. Say, now that we know each other again, maybe you would want to message me on my phone?** He typed his phone number out and sent it.

Eli waited a little bit before he received a ding.

> **Okay, cool. But please, don't give my number out to anyone. I'm not out.**

> **Oh yeah, I completely understand. Same here. Your secret is safe with me.**

Good, thanks so much.

Eli began to respond to him, but decided against it. He hoped that if his messages didn't resume on POF, then Christian would message him instead on his phone.

Several minutes had passed, and no response.

Just when Eli began to get desperate, and started typing out a message to resume talking to Christian, his phone lit up and vibrated, indicating a phone call.

Eli didn't recognize the number, which meant that it had to be Christian calling him. He didn't prefer talking on the phone, but when a guy as gorgeous as Christian was on the other line, he had no problem talking on it.

He picked up the phone and answered it before it went to voicemail. "Hello?"

"Hi," started masculine voice. *He has such a nice voice.* "Sorry I'm bombarding you with a phone call. I thought about messaging you, like you suggested, but I figured calling you would help us catch up quicker."

Eli smiled, and then realized that Christian couldn't notice it over the phone. "That's perfectly fine. Wow, it has been such a long time since we have seen each other."

"Yeah I know," responded Christian. "How long has it been exactly?"

"Around five years, I believe. What happened to you? Where did you go?"

"I never left Pinecrest," he said. "But it's a long story that I don't wanna bore you with now. I'll save it for if and when we meet in person."

He wants to meet in person?

"Yeah that's fine with me," agreed Eli. He paused, wondering what to say next. He couldn't just say "yeah" or "lol" to try to keep the conversation going, like he did with a text message. Right now, there was only dead air occurring between the two of them."

"So, what would you like to talk about?" He finally asked.

"I'm up for anything," Christian said. He said it so nonchalantly, as if he and Eli had been friends this entire time. Eli supposed it was okay to ask some more in depth questions.

"Okay," he started, hesitant about what he was going to say next, "so I was surprised to see you on POF. I didn't know this part about you when we were in high school."

Christian sighed, then said, "Yeah, well this is sorta of a new thing for me."

"Oh?" Eli questioned.

"Yeah," Christian continued, "I've just gotten over a breakup with my girlfriend recently. She was bad, like *really* bad. Anyways, the breakup tore me apart. What I used to think of as attractive, I then begun to think of as repulsive. I started thinking that every girl I came into contact with was just as big of a bitch as my girlfriend was."

Christian sighed. Eli could tell even over the phone that this had been a long ordeal for the man.

Christian began again, "I was at one of the lowest points of my life then. Then, out of the blue, I started noticing changes in me."

"Changes?"

"Yeah. I would go to the gym and while I would work out,

28

I would notice these guys, and I would get these weird feelings. Feelings I had never felt before with that gender. It freaked me out at first. But after awhile, I realized that maybe these feelings had always been there, but never noticed them until now."

Eli was amazed with his story. "Wow," he said, "that must had been an incredible change in your life. But you know, I have never really believed in labels, even though we live in the South. And I think that people can be attracted to the person, not their gender. In your case, this seems to be true."

"Maybe," Christian said. "But right now, I can't even imagine dating a girl right now. Kara really messed me up."

That means a better chance for me, Eli thought.

"What's your story?" Christian asked, brining the conversation back to Eli.

"Well, I've always have had an attraction to both guys and girls," Eli started. "But because of where we live, and my parent's possible reaction to the subject, I have never really felt comfortable in my own skin. It's been hard. But I've figured that whenever the right person comes along, male or female, I will know when to act on it. Even if it has to go against what everybody wants for me."

Christian had listened to Eli's whole story, and never once interrupted. "I know what you mean. I'm sorry you've been dealing with this for so long. So you had some idea when we were in school?"

"Yeah, I was starting to find it out."

"I would have never realized it. But at the same time, I didn't know you a whole lot back then. I mean, I kinda had problems distracting me. But that too, is a story for a later date."

"Oh, okay," said Eli. He had had hopes that he would be

able to find out why he went off the radar for so many years.

He guessed that he would have to talk about something else. "So, um, what exactly are you looking for?"

"Right now," Christian said, "just mainly friends, meeting new people, and maybe in the future, something more."

"Sounds like a good idea," Eli agreed.

"What about you?"

"Same, with the hopes of a relationship in the future."

"Nice," Christian said. "Well, I hope it works out for you."

"And the same to you."

They continued talking for several more minutes. In that time, Eli realized that they had more in common than what appeared on his profile. They both had gone to the same technical college before transferring to *Pinecrest University*. Christian was one year behind Eli, expecting to graduate in 2015. His plan was to graduate in computer technology, and after that, he didn't know.

Eli was really enjoying the conversation with Christian. *It has been so long since I have talked to a guy who hasn't asked me to show him a shirtless picture or has asked to hook up at this point.*

Eli knew that people like Christian were a rare breed. And cute ones like Christian were even rarer.

Christian's voice brought Eli back into the conversation.

"So, I think I'm going to get off of here and hit the old hay. Gotta run some errands in the morning."

"Oh okay. Well, I hope you have a great night."

"You too," Christian responded. "So, can I text you tomorrow? It has been a while since I have been able to hold a conversation with a person for this long."

"Oh yeah, certainly," Eli almost yelled, eager to make sure that the communication with Christian Lance didn't cease.

"Awesome! Well I look forward to talking to you then. Goodnight."

"Goodnight," Eli said.

The phone line went dead.

That was amazing.

Eli reminded himself to kiss Tori the next time he saw her. With any luck, she was going to be the reason he met the guy who was going to put all the other guys to shame.

He picked the phone back up again and started texting Tori, cramming in as many details as possible.

She's gonna wanna hear about this!

Chapter Three

Eli woke up in a good mood Saturday morning.

Not in a good mood. A great mood.

Never in the many years of pursuing love with a person has someone that he had talked to for the first time left an impression on him the way Christian had.

It had been almost impossible for him to go to sleep. He had been laying in his bed thinking of so many things to bring up in future conversation with his new acquaintance. Among those many things that he was thinking, he was simulating the first time he would see Christian, if he ever did get to see him. He imagined the two of them getting to know each other more over coffee or going to see a movie. And he couldn't stop thinking about how much different Christian looked.

God, he is so hot.

The alarm on his phone, which woke him up, was still ringing, bringing him back to earth and into the present. He turned it off and was greeted among several different messages.

Like usual, his phone had news updates that were sent from Twitter. Many people thought he was weird for agreeing to receive so many messages a day. But Eli would respond by saying that it kept him up-to-date with the world.

He continued scrolling through the messages, and starting noticing messages from real people.

Among them was Tori. Many messages that she had sent him overnight included: **Tell me who he is!?!** Of course, the details he had provided her about his encounter with Christian wasn't enough. She wanted to know his name, what he looked like, and any other juicy details that Eli might have captured. Eli had refused to tell her anything that he had promised Christian that he would not divulge. He knew she would continue to interrogate him when he arrived at *Arcade Hut* in an hour's time.

He put Tori out of his mind and continued scrolling down. The final message, which was sent earlier that morning, was from—

Christian!

Good morning, Friend :)

Eli's face immediately lit up. Usually, he was the one having to text someone and say good morning. But now, someone was saying go morning to him. *To him!*

Eli immediately texted back, hoping that too much time hadn't gone by since Christian had messaged him.

While he waited for a response, Eli got up and started getting dressed for work. He pulled out the black T-shirt with *Arcade Hut's* logo, and a pair of jeans that had a few holes in them. Since he had been working there for four years, the managers weren't as strict with his dress code as they were with the rookies.

Eli walked into the bathroom, with his phone clutched in his hand, and took a look at himself.

He didn't look too bad for a person who was lacking sleep and had bad bed hair.

He was shirtless, with sweatpants hugging the bottom part of his body, with the waistband of his *American Eagle* underwear showing. He couldn't help but look at his toned body, including the V-taper that had a small amount of hair trailing down his body.

It sounded conceited in Eli's head. He had always judged people for being in love with themselves and their bodies. But now that he had a body to be proud of, he felt like he deserved to applaud himself.

Christian's not the only one that has changed, thought Eli.

He checked his phone for a response from Christian. Nothing. But he did notice that he had spent more time admiring himself than he should have. He put the phone down and focused on getting ready for the day ahead.

***

Eli went downstairs and went into the kitchen, where the rest of the family was gathered. His father wasn't present, which meant that he had already departed for work. His mother was bent over the island counter, eating a bowl of cereal. His two sisters, Ruth and Carrie, had their backs turned, their eyes glued to the television.

His mother was already dressed. Diane Cooper was an early riser, which explained why she went to bed so early. Her hair was placed in a bun, and her makeup already put in place. Eli always told her that she had stood the test of time, if not looked better than when she was younger. He adored his mother, which was why he didn't want his secrets affecting their relationship.

"Good morning, Eli, " she said with a big smile on her face. "I was wondering if you were ever going to get up."

"When you work at *Arcade Hut*, you deserve to sleep in," Eli refuted.

"What time did you get in anyways?" she asked.

"Around 10:15," he said.

"Oh," she said, "I didn't even notice you came in."

"Shocking," he chuckled, mocking his mother and her weird sleeping schedule.

Carrie, his sister who was only a few years younger than he was, turned around from viewing the TV and addressed Eli. "She was hoping that you had stayed out and got some action."

Eli laughed in shock while his mother's eyes got big and eyed her daughter. "Carrie!"

"Sorry," she said, not realizing that she had said anything wrong. She flicked her shoulder-length hair in disgust of their opposition to her comment. "Mom was the one who was thinking it, not me."

Eli eyed her, and then turned his attention to his mother. He kept eye contact with her, waiting for an explanation.

"Well, it's true," Diane said. She put the cup of juice down on the counter to give him her full attention. "It couldn't hurt you to go and meet some new people." Her eyebrows went up, indicating that she had an immediate idea. "I know," she said, "why don't you go out with Tori? She would make a wonderful girlfriend."

Everyone looked at him, waiting for his reaction.

"No," he said immediately. "Tori is a dear friend of mine. She is like a sister to me." He looked at Carrie and said, "She's acts more like a sister than you sometimes."

Carrie stuck her tongue out at him and turned her attention back to the TV.

Diane got Eli's attention again by saying, "Eli, how are you supposed to find the love of your life if you don't take a chance at finding it? And even more importantly, how am I going to get any grandbabies if you don't find a good girl?"

"Oh God," Eli moaned, cringing.

"I'm sorry," she said. "But you're twenty-two years old. When I was your age, I was married, pregnant with you and had a car and house payment."

"Things have changed in the last twenty-two years," he said. He stopped, and then said, "You know, most parents would be glad that their kids aren't getting knocked up or getting someone knocked up. But you just can't wait until I get someone pregnant."

Diane ignored the laughing from Carrie and said, "Eli, " she placed her hand on top of his arm from across the granite counter top to keep him from walking away, "I am very glad that you haven't gotten anybody pregnant. Sure, you're not ready to have a child, but that doesn't mean that you can't start the journey that leads to that. I want you to be happy, and if you come straight home from work every night, I don't see that happening for you."

He walked around the counter next to his mom and said, "Thanks for the confidence, mom." He smiled, showing that he didn't take any offence to what she said. He kissed her on the cheek goodbye.

She kissed him back, "Have a great day, sweetie. And re-member; start finding your soul mate!"

Eli shut the door behind him and went down the back porch steps that lead to the driveway where his white Civic Hybrid sat. He got inside, and sat there for a second before turning the car on and putting it in reverse.

I wonder what they'd think if they knew the truth about me.

***

As soon as Eli made it through the front doors of *Arcade Hut* and made his way into the back offices to clock in, Tori was there to bombard him with questions.

"Tell me who it is," she exclaimed, jumping out of her chair. "You left me hanging last night, and it is all I can think about!"

Eli shook his head in opposition. "I told you," he said sternly, "He's not out. He asked me not to tell anybody, and I'm not going to."

"Ugh," she moaned, turning around and planting herself back in her seat. "You don't mind telling me that you are bisexual, but when you finally meet someone, you refuse to tell me anything about him." She folded her arms and put on the look that a child makes when they are ready to pout. "What good is having a best gay friend, if we can't trade stories on our love lives?"

"I'm not gay, first of all," he said, setting her straight, "I'm bi. And second, he isn't my lover. He's just a very attractive man who is not like any other man or woman I have ever encountered."

"Okay, he's not your lover," Tori conceded. "But you want him to be."

Eli sighed, knowing that she had a point there. He had only known the reoccurrence of Christian Lance for less than 12 hours, and already he was getting butterflies in his stomach and imagining how their fantasy relationship could be.

"Okay, you got me there," he said.

"Come on," she pleaded. "At least give me a picture. Something that'll let me know what you'll be dreaming about in the days to come."

Eli smiled, feeling the burning in his face starting to occur. It was true, he would probably be dreaming about Christian on many occasions.

"I can't risk it," he said, turning away from Tori and clocking in on the computer which was next door and opened the door out onto the work floor. "But I promise that you'll be the first person I tell if things get serious."

***

Unfortunately for Eli, his scheduled station was at the ticket exchange counter. There, he would spend grueling hours being a personal shopper for kids of all ages who were trading in their tickets for prizes. Those who had little tickets would spend most of their time fantasizing over prizes that were out of their price range, while the customers with a lot of tickets spend most of their time buying prizes that cost five tickets or less.

Eli was very professional at work, and promised to never use his phone in the workplace. For four years, none of the managers called him out on it, setting a standard that only a few were able to exceed.

But today, things were different. He was dying to pull his phone out and see if his new contact had messaged him. The thought of missing an important message from Christian was almost unbearable to Eli. And that feeling had been eating away at him for most of the day.

Eli finished the last customer in his line, saying farewell to the little girl who purchased the punching balloon and a massive amount of Fun Dip. The child's mother said thank you, leaving him surrounded by the thousands of dollars of cheap junk.

Nobody's around, Eli. Just go and see if he texted you.

He looked around the perimeter one more time. No managers were in sight. He knew Tori was in her office, but if she knew what he was about to do, she would encourage him to do it, even hoping that she would be able to watch him carry on the conversation. And towards the front of the building, the cashier was busy helping customers who would be coming to see him anywhere from several minutes to hours.

He decided that he couldn't wait any longer, and started making his way to a place in the facility more private.

He settled in on the ticket closet not too far away from his station, in case he was unexpectedly called back to help a customer.

Closing the door shut behind him, he made enough space for him in the makeshift closet that had been made even before his time at the arcade. He took extra security and held the doorknob with his hand, ensuring that no one would open the door and catching him texting on the job.

He pulled out his phone and scrolled through the many messages on his phone.

Yes!

There was a message from Christian, saying, **How is work going today?**

Eli responded quickly, not knowing how long he had to chat. **It could be better. I'd much rather be texting you instead of working here.**

A few seconds, and a response came back. **I wish you could do that too. Then you would be able to keep me company.**

Just say the word, Christian, and I'll quit my job right now and run over to keep you company.

Instead of speaking his mind, he said, **Aww, you're sweet.**

I try, Christian responded. **So...when are we going to hang out?**

Sweet Jesus! He wants to hang out! With me!

I'm not sure, Eli said. **When are you free?**

The time it took for Christian to respond was longer than his previous messages. Eli poked his head out the door to check and see if he had any customers.

There was one child with a big stack of tickets lying on the counter.

Just my luck.

Fortunately, Eli's phone vibrated in his hand with a response from Christian.

I don't know about you, but I'm free next Saturday night. How does that work for you?

Eli knew the answer to that without having to think about it. Like he had every other Saturday this month, he had to work a 12-8 floater shift. He didn't know why they couldn't just schedule him a double. Most of his day was already gone towards work anyways. He didn't know how late Christian would want to hang out, but for now, he was going to assume that he would be fine with Eli's schedule.

Sounds great, Eli said. **I have to go take care of some kid who won't leave my station. But I'll text you as soon as I am free.**

I'm looking forward to it, Christian responded.

Chapter Four

Saturday arrived quicker than Eli could have anticipated. And as the time neared closer, the more anxious he got about meeting Christian.

Every time Eli would meet a person online, they would start out seeming like they were *the one.* Then they would want to meet. And when Eli finally worked up the courage to meet them, he was let down because of the high expectations that he had set for each individual. Some of them were nice, but they weren't enough for Eli to continue pursuing anything more with them.

And Eli was afraid the same would happen with Christian.

This entire time, Christian sounded like the perfect guy. The more Eli talked to him, the more he realized that Christian was intelligent, thoughtful, funny and sweet. And above all, he was respectable. He never asked Eli to take off his shirt and send pictures of his chest, nor did he ask for anything worse than that. They never talked about sexual encounters or what they would do to each other if they finally met in person.

They did, however, talk about what it was like being attracted to the same sex in a town where that wasn't usually accepted. Christian would talk about how his father and step-mother were very judgmental, resulting in the decision not to come out to them. One night, Christian called and talked about an encounter that happened between him and his parents:

"So I went to *Cafe Stratta* to pick up dinner and saw that my dad and step-mom was also there, so I went and sat with them.

Apparently, I had walked in on a heated conversation, because they were discussing about how 'queers and illegal Mexicans are ruining the country'. It kinda stung a little so I proceeded to ask 'I understand that illegal Mexicans can have a negative effect on the economy due to not paying in to the system but, how exactly are gays ruining the country?'"

"What did she say back?" Eli asked.

"Well," Christian started, "Both my dad and her were like 'they want to be treated like married couples!' They said it like I was so stupid to even ask the question. That too stung."

Eli continued showing interest in his voice, showing Christian that he was eager to find out how he felt about what his parents thought about the gay community. "So did you say anything back?"

"I sure did," he said, confidently. "I didn't want to come out to them in spite of what they were saying, but the thought did cross my mind. It would have been priceless to have seen their faces when I told them that I was gay." Christian then sighed, returning from the thought that had apparently been consuming his mind for awhile. "Instead, I said, 'If you were in their shoes, wouldn't you like to be treated equally?' When they didn't say anything, I repeated my first question, 'So how are gays ruining the country if all they're trying to do is defend their right to love who they want to love?'"

"And what did they say to that?" Eli asked.

"Because they are," he muttered.

"I'm sorry?"

"My step-mom said 'because they are.'" Christian got quiet for a moment, leaving Eli on the phone wondering what his friend was thinking at that moment. "What kind of answer is that?" He resumed, not asking Eli in particular for an answer. "They were so ignorant, they were dead set against the idea of two men or women being in love, but couldn't back up their reason why they thought that way."

"I'm sorry," Eli said sympathetically. "It's not just them, though. A lot of people in Pinecrest feel that way."

"I know," Christian admitted. "But it would have been nice to know that my family could break away from the stereotypes of this place."

Eli could certainly agree with that. His family didn't speak badly of the gay community, nor did they make fun of anyone that they knew was gay in the area. But they did make little comments that made Eli question how they really felt about it.

Eli returned to the conversation with Christian, who was waiting for a response from him. "So, did you say anything else to them?" He asked.

"Very much against my will, I did not say anything else on the matter. I wonder if ignorance and blind hate has played a role in where society is today."

"I wouldn't doubt it," Eli said. "But you know, the world is changing very fast. People are becoming more accepting than they have ever been. I believe that even Pinecrest will one day embrace gay rights and allow everyone to be equal."

"If only it was happening now," Christian said with a less than optimistic tone.

That conversation had been playing in Eli's head for several days, questioning what his own family would say if they brought up the topic of gay marriage. He honestly couldn't imagine what they would say if he was to ever get up in front of them and say "I'm bi."

He tried not to think about the possible reactions that they would have towards his darkest secret. The idea of them not accepting him depressed him and made him unmotivated to do anything. And the idea that they would accept him, and he had been wasting his time living in fear of rejection, made him even more depressed.

On this Saturday, though, nothing could make him depressed. The thought of seeing Christian was able to carry him through the day. Even while working an 8-hour shift at *Arcade Hut*.

Eli came downstairs to a buzzing house. The rest of his family was taking a trip to South Carolina to meet relatives. While Eli had wished that he was able to go with his family, he was glad that they decided to go and visit today. That meant that he could meet Christian without having to be all secretive.

"Okay, Eli," his mother said, waving him towards her as she flung her purse around her shoulder. "Be good at work, and earn lots of money. Find something to entertain yourself when you get off work."

Eli immediately thought of Christian. "That won't be hard to do, mom."

His family kissed him goodbye and got in their Mercedes SUV before driving off towards the rising sun. Eli wasn't very far behind them, heading to a long day at work.

But at least he had something to look forward to.

***

"So, you're meeting your secret lover tonight?" Tori inquired from behind Eli as he was finishing a customer at the front desk.

"Yes," he said, keeping his attention on the paperwork that he was tending to. He still hadn't revealed the identity of his mystery friend, and he planned on keeping it that way. "I'm supposed to meet him after I get off work here."

"This is so exciting," she said, smiling so wide and trying very hard to conceal a squeal. "So what are you two going to do?"

"Going to dinner somewhere in town, I guess."

"Where?"

"I don't know," Eli said, realizing that they never talked about where they would actually want to eat at. He would have to remember to text Christian and ask what he would like.

"Well, what does he like to eat?" Tori asked, surprised that his night wasn't planned to the exact detail.

"I don't know."

"You don't know?" Tori gasped. Eli knew he was about to get an earful. "Eli, you gotta find out what he likes to eat, because—

"Alright, alright," he interrupted her. "I promise to do some research while I'm on break."

"Good," she said.

Their conversation was interrupted when a child behind the customer service desk yelled "EXCUSE ME!" several times.

"Damn kids," Tori said, rolling her eyes before turning around and walked to assist the child.

"I hope you're that nice when you have kids of your own," said Eli, chuckling.

Now that everybody was out of eyesight, Eli pulled out his phone from his pocket and checked to see if there was a message from Christian.

There was.

Looking forward to tonight, the message read.

Eli smiled. This was why he was in a good mood today.

You and me both, he responded.

***

Eli did what he promised Tori, and started researching what favorite foods Christian liked while he was on break.

He didn't want to just come right out and ask Christian what it was, because it would be clear that he was trying to plan where they would eat. Eli wanted to be cleverer than that. Maybe even romantic.

So he decided to look in the same location where they met: POF.

Eli never got tired reading about Christian in his profile. Every time he read it, he felt like he got to know the man a little bit better. And the more he got to know him, the more perfect he sounded.

While reading this time, however, Eli paid very close attention to what Christian's interests were. Now that he was trying to get to know him better, and have some prepared content ready for when they met that night, it couldn't hurt to research on a few more things about him.

I'm just an average guy, it started out. **I love computers, hence the computer technologies degree. I love any kind of anime. I'm a huge fan of the outdoors, so I love to hike, swim, or just do anything outside. Oh yeah, and I LOVE sushi!**

Sushi!

Eli wasn't a fan of that particular dish himself. But at least

46

he knew what his friend liked. This meant that he knew the location of their dinner spot tonight.

***

The crowd at *Arcade Hut* had come and gone by six o'clock. By that time, Eli was sitting at the front desk, impatiently waiting for eight o'clock to roll around.

He had texted Christian several times in the process, but there was no response from him.

Hopefully he's working on looking good tonight. Get real, Eli, like he would have to do anything to look good.

The thought of meeting Christian in two hours started to form knots in his stomach. Why was he so nervous?

In two hours, I'm either going to meet the hottest guy on the planet, or I'm going to meet a guy that I have set so high of a standard for, he is only going to disappoint me.

The thought began forming in Eli's head that maybe it was best that he called off the dinner meeting. It wouldn't be the first time he had called off meeting someone. He was very well known for it, and Eli knew it.

No, he thought. He didn't want to cancel on Christian. Christian had said multiple times that he was looking forward to dining with him and catching up. Eli didn't want to let him down.

And he didn't want to let himself down. For all he knew, he was considering giving up on possibly the best thing in his life. No, he would go through with meeting Christian and if Christian didn't interest him, then he would know that it was not meant to be, just like the other people that he had met in his life.

"Eli. "

He turned around at the calling of his name. Heading his way was Marie, the shift leader. Marie was a pretty girl, in her early thirties. Her reddish brown hair curled down below her shoulders and her teeth glistened like pearls. You couldn't tell that she had three children.

She was hired at*Arcade Hut* twelve years ago. She too was like Eli; wanting to pursue her college education, but also not afraid to climb the ladder of the business. Eli enjoyed working with her, and he felt that the feeling was mutual.

"Hi, Marie," he said, smiling as she approached him. He looked at her and said, "Not very busy tonight, is it?"

"No, I'm afraid not," she said with a sad look on her face. Eli supposed that she was just as enthused about being at work as he was.

Eli understood her situation. They both were working so hard to achieve their dreams, while working to earn money along the way. But no matter how hard you worked, or how many compliments you recieved while working there, it wasn't enough.

"So I've been looking at the labor costs," Marie said, "and I'm going to send somebody home. You've been here the longest today, so I thought I would ask you first if you wanted to go home early."

YES, Eli thought to himself. *Oh the joys of being the oldest employee on the payroll.*

Then a thought occurred to him.

Wait, that means that I'll be getting of two hours early. I wonder if Christian will be able to meet earlier than I told him.

Either way, Eli wasn't going to miss the opportunity to go home early and get as far away from the arcade as possible. "You bet," he said.

He rushed away from the front desk as fast as he could.

Eli texted Christian as soon as he clocked out. He was walking out the door when he typed **Just got off a few hours early. Wanna meet a little bit earlier than planned?**

He stood outside for a moment and considered waiting outside for a response. After few moments, Eli then decided to wait for a response in his car.

Thirty minutes passed by, and there was no response.

Maybe he is getting ready. Then a worse scenario went through Eli's mind. *Or maybe he is standing me up.*

After a few more minutes, Eli decided that he couldn't wait any longer, and decided to start driving home. He sure didn't want to stay in the parking lot of *Arcade Hut*, unless he was being paid.

If he doesn't respond to me by the time I get home, I'm not going back out. Maybe this is God's way of saying that it's not going to work out.

Eli passed the *Burger King* on the highway when more thoughts came flooding in.

No, Eli, you want to meet this guy badly. Don't sabotage yourself. Pull over and give him more time to respond.

And so he did. Parked in the *Burger King* parking lot was just as much fun as it was at his work.

Fortunately for him, he didn't have to wait long, because a text from Christian finally appeared on his phone.

Sorry about that, I've been doing some work outside. Oh wow, so you got off early. I wasn't expecting that. I don't mind meeting you early, but it'll take me a bit to get cleaned up. Where

would you like to go?

Eli already knew the answer to that. *Asian Palace.*

Christian responded. **Okay, that sounds good. But out of curiosity, why there?**

Because I know that you love sushi, and I think their buffet is the only place in town that is serving it this late.

Eli's phone vibrated a response. **It looks like someone has been studying up on my interests, ha-ha. Yeah, that sounds great. I'll meet you there in 30.**

Eli breathed a sigh of relief.

Aren't you glad you decided to wait a little bit longer?

***

It took Eli less than ten minutes to arrive in the parking lot of *Asian Palace,* since he was already in town.

And so he waited.

As thirty minutes started to come close, Eli's hands started to shake with anxiety. This happened every time he was ready to meet a new romantic prospect, boy or girl, for the first time.

To keep himself busy, and keep his mind off of his nerves, he started to pray.

"Lord," he started, "I'm not sure that you'll approve of this. A lot of people in this town say that you will smite all that decide to sin in homosexuality. But I don't believe them. I don't think that you care who we love, just as long as we have someone to love us back. So, I am here, right now, waiting to meet a guy, who in my head sounds absolutely perfect. I just pray that he meets my expectations and if he does, that you guide me to making sure that it works out, and give me the confidence to be proud of who I am, no matter who I decide to love. Amen."

Eli didn't think that many of those prayers were made by many people, but to him, he prayed a lot to keep him from going crazy in the judgmental town that he lived in.

A blue Nissan truck pulled up in front of him at that moment, causing Eli's stomach to turn upside down.

It's him.

Christian started getting out of the truck and pulled on a jacket to embrace the cold.

He looks so much better in person, he thought. *Well, I better get out there and say hey.*

Eli got out of his car and made eye contact with Christian. Once Christian spotted him, a smile spread across his face.

"Hello, friend," Christian said. His smile brought attention to his pearly white teeth, a great factor in Eli's book.

"Hi there," Eli said, returning his smile.

Christian came towards Eli and put a hand in front of him. Eli shook it, feeling the warmth coming from Christian's hand.

"It's good to see you, again," Christian said.

"It's good to see you too," Eli agreed, "I never thought I would be introducing myself to a classmate five years after we had class."

Christian laughed. Steam came out of his mouth as a result of the cold weather. "I guess we just do things backwards. But that's a good think. I like people that break out of the norm."

"Well you're in for a treat," Eli said, unable to contain a smile.

He is so handsome. And the way he talks, it's just amazing.

They started walking towards the restaurant. Neither of

them said anything for a few seconds.

"So how is school going?"

"I'm sorry?" Eli didn't understand the question.

"I asked how school is going for you," Christian repeated. "We go to the same university, don't we?"

"Oh yeah," Eli said, embarrassed. "School is great. I completely forgot that we went to the same school."

He talks like we have been friends for years.

"Yeah, it's a small world," Christian said. "Now, you mentioned that you were going into public relations, right?"

"Yeah," Eli was impressed by his memory. "I'll be graduating this May. And you are in computer technology?"

"Yep, and I'll be graduating next year."

"Yay us," Eli said. They both laughed, causing their breath to fog the restaurant door that they had now reached.

Before Eli could reach the door handle, Christian already had his hand on the handle and was pulling the door open.

"Thank you, sir," Eli said, entering the building.

"My pleasure," Christian responded.

Eli then decided to turn the tables on his new friend and rushed to the second door before Christian could get to it and return the favor.

"And a thank you to you, mister," Christian said, walking in.

"My pleasure," Eli said, repeating Christian's previous words.

They were seated across from each other, and their waiter went ahead and took their drink orders. Since it was a buffet, they got up and served themselves.

I can't believe I chose a buffet to meet someone for the first time, Eli thought.

His thought caused him to act, following Christian to pick up a plate. "Sorry it's not eloquent dining. The only reason I suggested this place was because they have sushi here. That, and because everyone else in town is closed at this hour."

"That's cool with me," Christian said, eyeing the sushi bar not too far way. "I love Asian food."

Eli nodded, and then went off in his own direction to get his own Asian favorites.

They both met back at the table, which now had their drinks sitting on top. "You picked some good stuff," Christian said, looking over on Eli's plate and seeing what he had picked.

"Thank you," Eli responded, showing his gratitude. "Yours looks good too, although I don't like the idea of eating sushi."

"Why is that?" Christian asked.

"Well, the thought of raw fish sickens me."

"First of all," Christian said, pointing his index finger at his plate, "This isn't real sushi."

"Huh?"

Christian chuckled, obviously amused that Eli didn't understand what he was saying. "This is imitation sushi. Totally not the same thing." He waited for Eli's understanding to appear on his face, which he got. Then he said, "And second, not all sushi is raw."

"Seriously?"

"Seriously," Christian responded. "There is some sushi that is raw, most sushi is made up of sticky rice, sea weed and vegetables.

It's really good."

"It certainly sounds yummy," Eli admitted. "I'll have to order it the next time I am offered real sushi, not the imitation stuff." He couldn't help but laugh.

Christian was laughing too.

The two of them engaged in small talk for a few minutes. Eli listened to Christian talk for his love of reading and hiking. While neither of those topics interested him, Eli hung on every word that Christian said. Eli kept eye contact with Christian the entire time, if not only to look at the bright green eyes that Christian was gifted with. Christian looked a lot like his picture that he sent Eli. He certainly had lost a lot of weight over the years. Under his *Abercrombie and Fitch* long sleeve shirt, it was evident that Christian had muscles, even more than what Eli had worked years for. Time had certainly been good to the man.

Once Christian's interest in his hobbies ended, they sat quietly and ate for a bit. A new conversation entered into Eli's mind, which caused him to speak up.

"So I have a question," he said after taking a sip of his Sprite and setting the cup down.

"Shoot," Christian responded, ready for what he was going to be asked.

"What happened to you in high school? I mean, one day you're there, and the next you're not."

"Oh yeah, that," Christian said, focusing his attention at the nearly empty plate in front of him. "I was miserable there, plain and simple."

"How so?"

Christian thought about it for a moment then said, "Well, I didn't have any friends. And the people who called themselves my friends only acted like it so they could tease and pick on me."

Eli was immediately reminded of Barry Grant.

God, how could I have been attracted to such a monster?

"I see," Eli said, not sure what else he could say.

"Yeah. The teachers were pretty much the same way. It was so bad that my grades were going down and I just wasn't happy there."

"So what did you do?" Eli asked, unsure where he could have went if he didn't go to the high school.

"I transferred to the school in the next county."

"Wasn't it hard for you commuting across counties?"

"Not really," Christian said, setting the record straight. "To be truthful, I had a blast there. I got along with everybody there, and the teachers were so helpful and kind. I had the highest grades there."

Eli pondered on this. All these years, Christian was still living in the same town as him, and he never knew it.

"Well I'm glad things worked out for you," Eli said, ending that topic on a positive note. "And you must be really smart. You're getting your degree in computer technology."

"Yeah, I love it. And I fix computers on the side, so that's how I pay my way through college."

"Very interesting."

"What about you?" Christian asked. "I don't believe I know all about what you are in school for."

"Well, I'm going for public relations. I fell in love with it during my senior project at high school, and after several pathway changes, I decided to pursue it as a career. And I'm glad I did."

"What do you want to use that degree for?" Christian questioned.

"Well, I've done a lot of PR for the school systems in the area. Actually, my internship that I did last summer was at the superintendent's office. I loved it. And they said that whenever they find the money, they want to hire me full time."

"That's great," Christian said, looking excited. "It must be really good to know that you have your life together and almost ready to graduate."

Eli shook his head in disagreement. "Nah, my life is far from together. Sure, on paper and in public, I look like the ideal employee and student, but when I'm by myself, I'm a mess."

Christian looked concerned. "Why is that?"

"Well," Eli stopped and leaned in and spoke at a whisper so nobody else could hear him, "Dealing with my preferences has been a difficult process. Sometimes I feel like there is happiness out there for me, and then sometimes I feel like I'm so screwed up that I'll never be able to find someone."

"Have you ever dated anybody, guy or girl?" Christian's voice was also at a whisper to respect Eli's privacy.

"Oh yeah," he responded. "But the thing is, nobody has ever felt right for me. And sometimes, I meet a great guy, and they don't want to see where things go because I'm not out. And then things don't work out with any girls because I get so confused when I'm around them. I've been dealing with this for years."

"I'm sorry about that," Christian said. And when Eli looked

at him, it was apparent that he was sorry for Eli.

"It's okay." Eli then decided to say something that would show his excitement in being in Christian's company. "It helps when I have people like you making me feel better."

Christian laughed, waving off Eli's compliment. "I'm nobody special, just somebody in the same boat as you."

"So what about you? How have you been able to deal with all this?"

"Is anybody able to deal with the situations we are in?" Christian asked, "Especially in a town such as Pinecrest?"

Eli shrugged, unsure of the answer, but knew that the chances were slim.

"But to answer your question," continued Christian, "I use an online forum for support."

"What's the site?"

"It's called equalitychat.com," Christian said. "It provides general chat, but also a place where you can ask for advice and get people's opinions from all over the world. It has certainly helped me over the last few months."

"It sounds helpful," Eli said, nodding his head. "I might have to look at it sometime."

The rest of the dinner was filled with small talk. They talked about Eli's four year employment at *Arcade Hut* and the many stories that have come from both Eli's and Christian's personal experiences from there. It was clear that Christian wasn't a fan of the place either, and wished Eli the best of luck in getting out of there as soon as possible.

Christian looked down at his watch and groaned. "I better

head home and get to bed. I tend to be an early sleeper and an early riser."

"Bless you," Eli said. "Because I certainly couldn't do that." Eli was more of a night owl.

So they both got up. Before Eli could reach for the check that the waiter had left on their table half an hour ago, Christian snatched it up and put it out of Eli's reach.

"Please," Eli pleaded, "this is my treat."

"No, this is *my* treat."

It didn't look like there was any way that Eli was going to talk him out of it. So he conceded and let Christian head to the cash register to pay. Eli instead took care of the tip and walked up towards Christian.

"Thank you so much," he said. "You really didn't have to do that."

"It was my pleasure," Christian said, grinning. "But you're paying next time."

"It's a deal."

Christian thanked the cashier and held the door open for Eli.

Eli thanked him and entered the cold atmosphere. He forgot how cold it was tonight. He wasn't smart, like Christian, and brought a jacket with him.

"Do you hike?"

Eli turned around to Christian's voice and saw him putting on his jacket. Christian was waiting for an answer.

"It's been years," Eli said. "I'm not that big on outdoors—" He hoped he didn't turn Christian off by that comment. "—but I would love to try it sometime."

"Awesome!" Christian was excited that Eli was willing to try it. "Once it warms up, I'll mention it again."

Christian held out his hand for another handshake. Eli took it, once again taking advantage of the warmth that Christian radiated off of him.

"I had a blast," Christian said. "We will definitely have to hang out again."

"I agree," Eli said, shaking his head in agreement. "And we will."

"You have a goodnight."

"You too," Eli said, already regretting that they had to depart so soon.

Christian got into his blue Nissan and started driving away, leaving a trace of his existence with a cloud of exhaust.

Eli stood out in the cold and watched Christian drive away into darkness.

But Eli wasn't cold. Instead, he felt warm inside.

Even though they had met only once, Eli already came to a conclusion.

He's the one.

Chapter Five

"There is certainly something wrong with you, Eli. "

"I'm sorry, I don't know what you mean."

The whole family was surrounded around the table, eating breakfast before they drove off to church. Eli came down cheerful and greeted everybody with a warm "Hello." Eli thought that his family would welcome his new attitude, since he was usually grumpy waking up early on a Sunday morning.

Apparently, he was wrong.

"You're so happy," his mother said. "Are you okay?"

How was he going to cover this up? He wasn't ready to tell them that he went to dinner with an attractive person. A man. A man named Christian.

"I just had a good day at work last night. You know those don't come often."

They bought his excuse and went back to their breakfast. Everyone but his sister, Carrie.

"If I didn't know any better, I would think you got laid."

"Carrie," everyone in the house yelled.

"What?" She asked, once again unsure what she had done wrong.

Eli's mother decided to answer for her. "We don't want to hear things like that about your brother."

"That and they're so tired trying to keep up with your promiscuity that they don't have time to worry about my nonexistent love life," Eli threw back at his sister.

This got an "OOOOOOO" out of Ruth, who was sitting next to Eli.

Eli's comment angered Carrie so much that she grabbed a handful of cereal from the nearby box and threw it at him.

"HEY!" Exclaimed Eli.

"Enough!"

Everybody was silent after hearing Eli's father.

"Exactly," Diane said. "Now, let's get in the car, and get you two to the altar."

"Yeah," Eli muttered, "so Carrie can cleanse her soul."

His comment still wasn't quite enough to escape Carrie's ears, who returned with a line of insults towards him.

***

Before the church service began, Eli pulled his phone out and texted Christian.

I had a blast last night.

They didn't talk much after leaving *Asian Palace*. Christian went straight to bed, while Eli waited up for his family to return from South Carolina, as well as reflect on how well his night went with Christian.

Was it a date? Or were we just two friends hanging out?

He paid for dinner. Does that make him extremely romantic or just very generous with his friends?

Eli was unsure what it meant for the two of them. But for Eli, he hoped that it meant something more than friendship. Never in his life did he get such a great feeling inside after meeting a person for the very first time. And never in his life did he ever feel so *free*, like it didn't matter to him what people thought when they saw him with another man.

He looked down to see if there was a response on his phone. Nothing.

Eli figured as much. Christian was probably still sleeping, or was doing some morning chores. Hopefully he would have a response waiting for him by the time the service was over.

The choir director took to the pulpit and put the microphone towards his mouth.

"Good morning everyone," he said. He waited for members of the congregation to respond the same to him. "Isn't it good to be in the Lord's house today?"

Eli shook his head in agreement. For the first time in a long time, he felt like he had something to be grateful for.

"Let us stand," the director said, motioning with his hands for the crowd to rise from their seats. Eli rose from his seat next to his family on the back pew.

Music started to play, and the choir members began clapping their hands in rhythm of the beat.

Eli began clapping with the same rhythm, celebrating anything and everything.

***

There was still no reply from Christian by the time Eli and his family had arrived home. Eli wasn't too worried about it, but the thought of Christian no longer wanting to talk to him after their outing was in the back of his mind.

Once lunch was made, everybody went into different areas of the house. Diane and Charlie went into the main living room to watch the race that was currently taking place. Eli's sisters went into another room to watch their shows. And Eli went and ate in his room, a place that was void of TV or game consoles. It was just him, his music and his computer.

Eli placed himself in the chair facing the computer desk. His plates of fried chicken nuggets were in front of him. He then turned on his computer and started playing a variety of Tori Amos songs.

He really wanted to talk to Christian. It seemed weird to Eli, maybe even pathetic, but things felt weird to him when he wasn't talking to this new person in his life.

Then a thought occurred to him.

He remembered the conversation Christian and he had the night before about the site he used for support dealing with his "forbidden" attraction. What was it called again?

www.equalitychat.com

Eli was glad that the thought occurred to him. Even though he wasn't able to talk to Christian at that moment, he would be able to understand him better by reading his posts on the site.

He clicked open his browser and typed in the address. The site that he was directed to was a page full of blue and white, and hundreds of thousands of posts full of text.

Where do I even begin?

He needed to narrow the posts down to just the posts that Christian had made. Up at the top of the page, Eli found a search bar. Remembering his username from POF, Eli typed in techgeek4 and hit SEARCH.

Up came a page full of posts that were made by Christian. Eli read previews of each post to see which one would be most worthwhile. He wasn't worried about missing anything important, because he would make sure to read every post in the future.

Eli searched all the way down to the bottom of the page, where one of Christian's first posts was made. He clicked on it, and started to read the content.

A year ago I would have identified myself as straight. I was dating a beautiful girl and things were going well. I couldn't imagine my life without her. I had even thought about proposing to her. But when things got too difficult, she walked away, and I haven't heard from her since. I was crushed, and I never thought that I could love again.

While he was aware of the major details, the minor details in Christian's post made Eli feel like he had found the entrance into the man's soul.

I was incredibly lonely for what seemed like forever. I was so desperate, I kept trying to beg for her to be in my life again. She said things that are now unforgiveable, and I haven't tried to make contact with her in over a year. I have no attraction towards females anymore. While I understand not all girls are like this, in fact, few are like this, I have thought about the circumstances and I have revisited the past year over and over and I've realized that things will never be the same.

Wow, Eli thought, *it sounds like he really loved her.*

It was about four months after our breakup when I started taking notice of guys when going into a gym, or on the trail at campus. Feelings started to form, feelings I had for the fairer sex previously which now had swapped.

Eli was reading the post very carefully, making sure not

to miss a word or phrase. Christian hadn't told him these things. It occurred to Eli that maybe Christian wasn't ready to share this in-depth story with the male gender, particularly a guy that he has only spoken to for a week.

He continued reading.

It finally came to the point where I couldn't stop thinking about it. Thoughts of the same sex were with me whereever I would go. Whether it was at school, at the gym, or in my dreams. I was beginning to think that I was crazy, and considered going to a psychiatrist.

It pained Eli to read the hurt bleeding through the text that Christian had typed out. Remembering the dinner that they shared together, he didn't see any of this pain. He seemed too peppy and full of personality. This post was really opening Eli's eyes to the fact that even Christian wasn't immune to the confusion and fear of judgment that everyone felt when confronting their sexuality.

The dreams; dreams of men touching me, kissing me, and me wanting to do the same, have left me overwhelmed. I know now that this was a side of me that I never explored, and I now need to embrace it. I felt more alone that ever before. But now, I feel liberated and eager to find out what lies in store for me.

The second-to-last sentence of the post broke Eli's heart. Fortunately, he was relieved to read the positive attitude that Christian had for himself.

He continued scrolling down the page, reading the posts that fellow forum members had to say about Christian's situation. The majority gave comforting advice, saying that maybe that his feelings for the same sex had always been there and the traumatic incident with his ex-girlfriend forced these feelings to light.

Eli agreed with what they said to Christian. He couldn't help going back to what Christian said earlier in his post.

No, Christian doesn't need to go see a psychiatrist. He isn't crazy. He is, however, driving me crazy by making me realize that he is not only all the things that I noticed at dinner, but he is also sensitive, which is a very rare thing for guys in Pinecrest.

It took every bit of restraint in him to keep from texting Christian and beg him to tell him all of his troubles. That, and from proposing to him.

He has to be the one, Eli thought. *And I need him to realize that I am interested in him before someone else realizes the same thing and tries to snatch him up.*

Eli's phone vibrated next to the computer, startling him. He picked it up and starting feeling knots in his stomach again.

Hi there, sorry for the late response, I decided to take a hike up the road, read a post from Christian.

Eli was confused by what he said, but was also happy that Christian had finally responded to him.

Hey there! You're fine, I'm just glad you are responding. I thought you said that it was too cold to go hiking?"

It is, Christian texted back, **But I love it so much that I can't avoid it. So I insulated myself enough for the trip. I'm just now getting back.**

He is sure dedicated to his physical activities.

Well I'm glad you had a good hike.

Christian responded with **Me too. And yes, I had a blast with you last night.**

That message caused Eli's heart to beat faster, and his face to blush.

No one has ever made me feel this way before.

He couldn't resist, and responded with a message that connected to last night's meeting.

Yeah, it was perfect, he began, then typed, **Now I owe you a date lol.**

After he sent it, Eli wasn't sure if it was the right thing to do. Either Christian would take him up on the offer, or set the record straight that he wasn't into him.

A couple of minutes passed, and there was no response from Christian. Either he was texting a long message back, or he was contemplating how to put Eli down easy, or just decided to ignore him all together. Eli hoped he hadn't shot himself in the foot.

After a few more minutes, Eli's phone finally vibrated in response to Christian's message. Eli wasted no time in seeing what he said.

I don't know if I'm ready for a "date," Christian responded. **But I would sure love to hang out again.**

Well, he didn't flat out say "no."

I understand, Eli typed. **Maybe we could go hiking soon.**

That sounds great. We can do it as soon as it warms up.

Eli responded his agreement.

He couldn't help it; he was disappointed that Christian didn't recognize their dinner last night as a date. But, on the plus side, he said that he wasn't ready for that. That meant that there was still a chance for things to work out in Eli's favor.

Was there still a chance?

Chapter Six

As time passed, the days were getting longer and warmer. And Eli didn't forget that Christian had promised that time to go hiking was vastly approaching.

In the couple of weeks that followed their first meeting, the two continued to message each other. And on a couple of occasions, Eli and Christian met up to walk around the walkway in Pinecrest. There, they would continue talking about nothing in general; usually talking about what they were reading, watching, or playing on their consoles. Eli never mentioned "dates" again, deciding that if and when Christian wanted to go on a date, he would tell him.

On Saturday, Eli had made plans with Christian as soon as he was off from work. Like the other Saturdays, Eli was working most of the day. He was relieved though to find out that he was a floater, someone who would go from station to station making sure that everybody had had their break, that all the games were replenished with tickets, and that customers were helped when the other employees were busy with other things.

Six o'clock rolled around, and it didn't look like Eli would be lucky and get off early for a second time. But even though he still had two hours left to go, he still had something to look forward to; seeing Christian.

Eli was standing at the front desk, covering for another employee when a large party walked through the doors and walked towards him.

"Hello," Eli said with a smile on his face. Even though he

despised the place, and knew that he was working for less than what he deserved, he always acted as professional as possible, putting any personal problems aside and putting the customer's needs first.

Among the many people in the group, the oldest woman stepped forward. She was a heavyset woman, who had blonde hair that was fading to white. Her face didn't hold a wrinkle, which indicated either that she took really good care of herself, or she had enough money to get herself fixed.

"How may I help you?" Eli was still smiling. It was already obvious that the woman wasn't together at all. She was either trying to organize herself from the trip with her family, or she was just not a very nice person.

"Can you please hold on?" She asked irritably, unhappy that Eli had asked to assist her before she was ready.

Eli knew quickly that it was going to be a long ordeal with this crowd.

When she was ready, she finally acknowledged Eli, saying that she had never been there before and needed an explanation on how everything worked.

After several minutes, and several interruptions from the woman, her husband, and the rest of the family, Eli was able to explain how the arcade worked.

The woman pointed down at one of the promotional flyers that was taped to the counter. "What's this flyer?" She interrogated, and then looked at him, upset. "Why haven't you offered us this package?"

"Ma'am, I said at the beginning that that special only qualified for people with a group of twenty or more." He looked back towards her party, and then looked back at her. "And you clearly don't have that many people."

"Well I wish you would have explained it better to us." She turned to her husband and spoke loud enough so Eli could hear it, "He's not explaining it to me right."

Eli kept his cool, knowing that he had said everything the way it was supposed to be said and that he had even "dumbed" it down for the woman who was impossible to please.

A younger man from the party walked up towards the old woman and her husband. He either was their son or the son-in-law. Either way, it was clear that he had learned their same demeanor.

"Kid, just give it to us straight, what is the best deal for us?"

Kid? Who are you calling kid?

Eli once again explained what he thought the best deal was for them, and what all they could do with that package. After he was finished, he watched the family debate on what they should purchase.

The younger man turned back around to Eli and said, "Look, let's just get forty dollars worth of stuff and see where that gets us."

The man looked at the older woman and waited for her to pay. The woman, shook her head in disgust. "Forty dollars for games? That is outrageous." She looked up at Eli. "You all should be ashamed for charging so much for little kids to play."

"I'm sorry," Eli responded. "I don't make up the prices."

Nobody responded, not paying any attention to him or what he was saying. Instead, they were looking at the bowling alley that was a few hundred steps away.

Please, don't let them ask to do bowling.

The bowling alley at *Arcade Hut* was one of the many reasons why he hated working there. When the building was renovated to accommodate the arcade, they purchased one of the oldest bowling systems known to man. For years, they spent thousands of dollars upgrading the parts and television screens. But they wouldn't cave and hire a full-time pin jockey to repair the lanes as soon as they broke down. So, as a result, the lanes would break, and they would never get fixed.

As of that moment, Eli knew that only five lanes were working. And there was no guarantee how long they would last.

"Can we do bowling?"

Eli made eye contact with the woman, who was already making her way to the lanes.

"I'm sorry, ma'am, but all of the lanes are currently full."

The family looked that the empty lanes, then turned back to Eli, giving him a look like he was blind.

"What do you mean they are full?" Asked the older man, with an agitated voice. "There are five lanes that aren't being used."

"I'm aware of that, sir," said Eli. "But half of the lanes are not working. So I have to put you down on a waiting list. When we call you on the intercom, you can come up and play."

Everybody rolled their eyes.

That's strike two, Eli realized.

Somebody that hadn't already burnt up their patience with Eli came to him to put their names down. They asked how long it would be until they got to play. Eli told them that based on what was on the sheet, it would be forty minutes. Even that agitated the family member, but they put their name down and walked away.

"Who was that?" Kara asked, walking up towards him. Kara was another employee at *Arcade Hut* who had worked there for a year. She had been gone a while, helping a customer get his proper amount of tickets.

"Thank God you're back," Eli said, sighing in relief.

"What is it?"

"Crazy people," he said, pointing towards the family that he just served. "Make sure to watch out for them."

Kara nodded as Eli walked away and started heading to another station.

Hopefully, he wouldn't have to deal with those people again.

***

Eli started walking back towards the front at 7:30. Only thirty more minutes, and he would be able to get off work and go hang out with Christian.

The thought was sounding better and better as time passed.

He had worked extra hard to avoid the obnoxious family that had had several problems with him. They came towards the back several times, playing the smaller games for the kids.

Did they ever go and play bowling?

As he walked by the front door, he noticed that it was raining heavily.

Great, now Christian and I can't hang out outside.

"Excuse me!"

Eli, who had been staring out the front door, turned and saw the old woman, walking towards him, slowly but surely. Her face did not look pleasant. Eli wondered if it ever did.

Eli gritted his teeth and attempted at a smile. "Yes ma'am," he said, "What can I help you with?"

The woman put her hands on her wide hips. "You can tell me when we are going to be called to bowl."

"Yes, of course," he started heading to the front desk. "Let's go take a look and see."

As Eli was walking to the front desk, he noticed that there were only two lanes running. Either the previous players had left, or the lanes were now not working.

He hoped it was the first scenario.

He walked to the bowling computer, which was directly across from the front desk, right next to the bowling lanes. He looked closely and noticed that lanes five, seven, and eight, the lanes that were previously used, were labeled "OUT OF ORDER".

Great. Just great.

Eli looked around to see if Kara was nearby. Where was she? He hoped that she would return to the front soon so she could explain both to him and the irritable customer why they hadn't been called. In the meantime, he was going to have to play it by ear.

"Ma'am," he said, bringing her attention back to him. She walked closer to the desk, ready for an explanation. "I apologize in advance for this. But it seems that three lanes have went out since you were last here, and the two remaining lanes still have the same people on it who were here when you put your name down. I don't know why, but they're still there."

The woman looked at the lanes to confirm his story. When it checked out, she looked at him and asked, "Well, when will we be able to play?"

"Well, that's the problem," he responded. "Nobody on this

list has been called to come up and play, and your party is fourth on the list. It'll be another forty minutes."

She shook her head, not accepting his excuse. "No," she said, shaking her pudgy finger at him, "No, this unacceptable. You promised us that it would take forty minutes, and now we come up here an hour and a half after we sign up, and you're now telling us that it'll be another forty? No, what kind of business are you running here?"

Eli anticipated that response. He had foreseen it ever since her and her family walked in through the front doors.

"I apologize for the inconvenience," he said, watching her still shake her head in anger. "I'm just a floater, so I'm only up here every once in awhile, so I don't know why we are in this situation or what has happened to put us in this situation. But, I certainly didn't foresee this when I gave you that estimate."

At that moment, Kara walked up and stood next to Eli as he was explaining this to the red beet of a woman who looked like she was ready to explode with anger.

"Is everything okay?" Kara asked to no one in particular.

Before Eli could explain to her, the woman said, "No, things are not okay." She pointed to Eli and continued. "Because HE promised us that we could bowl a long time ago, we are now being told it will be even longer because your lanes aren't working. So maybe you can be more helpful than he has been."

Eli could feel his skin getting hot. Very rarely had he lost his temper in front of a customer, and he could feel his limit being reached.

Kara took her turn to explain. "I too am aware of the

problem. Since Eli signed your party up, we have had three lanes shut down on us. We have no repairman on staff to fix them, and none of the employees working right now are trained to go back and fix them. So right now, we only have two lanes available." She motioned towards Eli and said, "Eli had no knowledge of this, nor would he have signed you up if he knew this would occur."

Eli felt like he could kiss Kara at that moment. He hadn't worked with her much since she was hired a year ago. But right then and there, he noticed that she was a great employee, and was someone that would be able to stand by his side without throwing him under the bus.

"That is still unacceptable," the woman said, still shaking her finger at them. "You promised us that we would be able to play at a certain time, now you are going back on your word. You are a liar, and had I known this when we first came in, I would have taken my money and went elsewhere."

How dare this fat bitch call me a liar?!

At that moment, one group that was vacating a lane put their shoes on the counter and walked away. An idea then struck Eli.

Eli turned to Kara and spoke up so the woman could hear their conversation.

"What if we just let them go right now so that there won't be any more problems?"

"No," Kara flat out said. "I know that they have been inconvenienced, and I'm sorry about that. But there are three other groups that have been waiting just as long as she has, and I'm not going to let them go ahead of the line just because they decided to pitch a fit."

Kara did have a point there.

Eli turned back to the old woman and shook his head apologetically. He didn't know what else to say to her.

"Again, I apologize for this," Eli said, feeling his face getting red.

"You have said sorry all night, and I'm done hearing it from you," she said. "I want a refund."

Eli and Kara both looked at each other. Then Eli said, "I'm sorry, ma'am, but you haven't paid for bowling yet."

"I don't care," she said, folding her arms around her chest, refusing to leave. "I want all of the money I paid you back."

Eli sighed in anger. He wasn't going to fix this with her.

"Ma'am, it is clear that I can no longer help you. I'm afraid I'm going to have to get my manager to assist you from this point on."

"Very good," she said, smiling. "Maybe someone can finally help me out."

Eli turned towards Kara and said, "I'm going to go grab Marie."

Fortunately for him, Marie was just down at the prize counter. He walked down there next to her. She was helping out a customer when she noticed that Eli was right next to her.

"What's up?" she asked. She knew that when Eli came up to her asking for help, it was because no one else but her could do it.

"I have a customer that is unhappy because she hasn't been able to get into bowling yet," he started, pointing towards the front desk. "I have apologized numerous times for not being able to get her in there, but with the lanes breaking down, their wait time keeps getting pushed back."

He made a grab for the remote that scanned the tickets and the prizes. "I can take care of this if you want to go and talk to her."

She nodded, handed him the remote and started heading up towards the front. Eli hated to bring another person into the situation, but he was sure Marie was used to it. She had numerous complaints to deal with every day.

Eli had taken care of multiple of customers when Marie walked towards him, clearly more stressed than when she first left.

"I just need to clarify what happened," Marie said. "She says that you promised her only a forty minute wait when it turned out to be longer than that. She said that you lied about it." She put a hand on his shoulder. "I know you wouldn't lie about something like that, but please, tell me your story."

Eli took a deep breath and quickly recollected in his mind what happened. "They came in, and after a while of choosing packages, they decided that they wanted to do bowling. At the time, we had five lanes, so I told them that based on the waiting list, it would be a forty minute wait. Then I left the desk and floated to other stations. In between me leaving and me coming back up front, there were three more lanes that went out. She asked me what the wait was, and I told her that there were still people waiting, and that it would take more time to get them in."

Marie nodded. "Okay," she said. Then she turned around and headed back up to the front.

Several more minutes passed, and Eli served several more customers while he waited for Marie to return. Eventually, the line had dissolved and he stood there, waiting for her.

When she did walk back up to him, he thought that the

situation was finally over.

"I am so sorry that you had to go through with that. I thought I was able to contain the situation on my own, but they wouldn't accept any of my apologies."

Marie nodded, but she looked as if there was something else that had to be said.

At that moment, he noticed the younger man that he had dealt with at the same time as the old man and woman appear near the prize counter.

It isn't over.

"So I gave them a full refund," Marie started. "But they refuse to leave until you give them an apology."

The nerve of these people.

Eli responded with a confused look on his face. "I've apologized to them multiple times. What will make this time any different?"

"Well, they say one of the kids is crying because he didn't get to go bowling. They want you to apologize to him."

Eli couldn't believe what he was hearing. The people were crazier than he thought.

"I don't know about that, Marie. I mean, I did absolutely nothing wrong."

Marie understood why he was hesitant and said, "I understand why you wouldn't want to. And it's true, you didn't do anything wrong. But at the same time, we did inconvenience them by signing them up for something that they won't get to play. It's just good customer service if we do this. And I'll be right there next to you to defend you."

Eli thought about it long and hard. These people didn't deserve anything that Eli gave them. But at the same time, it wasn't the kid's fault that he was born from complete idiots. And Marie was right; it was good customer service, something that he always strived for.

"Okay, I'll do it."

"Thanks, Eli. "

Eli took a deep breath and started walking up towards the front. As he started walking, he noticed that the man was still standing next to the counter. He had been waiting for Marie to finish talking to Eli.

The man pointed at Eli. "You. Up front. Now."

Eli nodded his head in response. "Yes, sir."

You are not going to bend over and take it, Eli. You are going to do the professional thing, but you are not going to take any of their crap.

He reached the front counter with Kara behind him, and Marie standing next to him.

As soon as he spotted the old woman, he gave a big apologetic smile and said, "Once again, I am very sorry for the confusion. If there was anything that I could do to make your visit better, I would do it."

"Oh no," she said, waving her finger again, "don't apologize to me. I'm done hearing that you're sorry when you obviously are not."

The man reached the front desk, huffing. "So here's the deal," he started, looking Eli straight in the eyes. Eli never beated an eye for a second. "I'm going to get my son up here, and you are going to apologize for lying to him by promising him that he could do something and then turn around and say that he couldn't."

The old woman next to him smiled and nodded, hanging on every word. She was glad that Eli was going through this.

"I mean, the kid is crying," he continued. "And anybody that causes a child to cry at a place like this deserves to go up to him and face the guilt that they deserve."

The man walked away, leaving Eli, Marie and Kara standing there, waiting for the next round this absurd family had in store for them.

Not very long after he walked away, the man started walking back up towards the front, with a small child in tow. Once they reached the front desk, the father picked up the child and flung him onto the counter, causing many things on the desk to fall over.

They are loving every minute of this show they are putting on, Eli thought.

"Now," the man said, addressing his child and pointing at Eli, "this is the man that ruined your evening, and he has something he wants to say to you." Then he addressed Eli and pointed at the kid. "And you, you are going to look him in the eyes and apologize to him."

Eli nodded, turning away from the man that was putting him in such an uncomfortable position. He could feel himself about to burst. It was going to take all the strength that he had from losing it then and there.

He looked at the child. The young boy must have been five or six. With his blonde hair, he looked very cute. He didn't see any indication that the child had been crying. Probably a lie that the father told to make Eli feel horrible. It was such a shame that the child had to live a life with these awful people.

Eli looked him straight in the eyes, not because the father told him to, but because he was truly sorry for any child that was upset because of something he may have done or was accused of doing.

"Hey buddy," he started out, reaching his hand out towards the end of the counter so it looked like he was making an authentic attempt at apologizing. "I want to apologize because you didn't get to play bowling. It is my job to make sure that you have a great time here. And obviously, I didn't do that today. I hope you will forgive me, and understand that I would never do anything to intentionally make you upset. Okay buddy?"

The child nodded back at him. To Eli, it looked like the kid didn't have any idea why he was getting an apology.

Eli could feel the sobbing begin deep within himself. He had to keep it in long enough until they left. He promised himself that he was going to be strong, but he could feel himself breaking down inside.

"Okay, that's better," the father said, walking away.

The old woman picked her grandson from the counter, and then held him in her arms.

"Now," she said, speaking to the child and pointing at Eli, "Tell him that you forgive him, and ask him to never ruin a child's day the way he ruined yours."

Eli's insides turned upside down. The old woman had won. And she won by striking one last devastating blow to Eli's spirit.

He remained speechless, while Marie and Kara gasped in shock and disgust.

Whether the young boy actually did what his grandmother told him to do, Eli didn't know. The old woman hurriedly turned around and starting walking towards the front door.

I would be that mean if I was that ugly, Eli thought.

He didn't have time to think for too long. He could feel tears escaping from his ducts. The sobbing began to affect his breathing. And his lip started to quiver uncontrollably.

"That was the hardest thing I have ever had to do," Eli squeaked out, wiping his eyes so the two women couldn't see him in such a vulnerable state.

"Eli," Marie said, embracing him in a hug, "You did well right there. Not many people would have been able to handle that situation the way you did. You kept your cool, and you gave them an apology that they didn't deserve. This is why you are our best employee."

Those words made Eli sob even more. "Then why do I feel like the worst person in the world?"

A customer walked up towards the front. Kara went to the desk to assist them while Marie assisted someone at the bowling alley.

"I need to take a breather," he said to no one in particular as he started heading to the closet next to the front desk, grabbing some napkins along the way.

Inside the closet, he let all of his emotions out, unable to contain the flood of tears that he had been holding back.

You bent over and took it. You stupid idiot!

Eli stood there for several minutes, wiping the tears away as he replayed every second of that incident. He couldn't help but question what else he could have said to honor his dignity and not have allowed that family to humiliate him in front of his co-workers. How was he ever expected to come back to work again?

Eli pulled his phone out to check the time. It was 7:40. Only twenty more minutes until he was allowed to break away from this prison.

Then it hit Eli that he still had to meet Christian right after work.

There is no way I'm going to be able to hang out with him in this shape.

Eli opened up a blank message and texted Christian.

I don't think I'm going to be able to hang tonight.

He put the phone back in his pocket and reached for the door. He felt as good as he was going to get. Just well enough to slither out of the building.

When he returned to the front desk, Kara and Marie were both there, waiting for him. Kara was first to reach him, grabbing him in a big hug. "You were amazing, Eli. I'm so proud of you. I wouldn't have been able to do what you did."

Eli nodded his thanks, even though her words were no comfort to him.

Marie was right next to Kara, looking way worse than when Eli first pulled her aside to take care of the incident.

"Eli, it says that you are supposed to get off at eight, but I want you to leave a few minutes early. You certainly deserve it." Kara shook her head in agreement.

"I'll take you up on that," he said, a small sob still able to escape his mouth.

He turned away from them and walked towards of the back of the building where the offices were. He walked at a brisk pace, hoping that nobody would come up to him asking for assistance, or a co-worker asking what was wrong.

As he was clocking out, he felt his phone vibrating against his leg. He pulled it out and saw a message from Christian.

Aww, why? I was really looking forward to it.

Hearing that Christian wanted to see him made him feel even worse.

Damn you, old hag, for ruining my night.

It was a rough day at work. I mean, really bad. I'm actually crying right now, it was so bad.

He walked out of the office and towards the front door.

When he got close to the door, he noticed that the family was still there, waiting for the rest of their party to meet them. Eli walked to his right, away from the door. There was no way he was going to give them another opportunity to humiliate him. So he went out the side door, which allowed him to avoid contact with anyone else.

By the time he reached his car, he was already soaked from the heavy rain outside. As soon as he got inside, he starting the sobbing and crying again.

Why are you letting those idiots get to you? You have dealt with crazy people for four years, and you decide to let people like that get to you?

A response from Christian lit up his phone.

Oh no!! What happened? Do you need to talk?

Reading Christian's concerns made Eli even more upset. The incident had even taken away the joy of reading a message from Christian.

I'd love to talk, Eli responded. **But I'm in such a mess; I**

wouldn't want you to see me like this.

He got a response almost instantly.

I don't care. Meet me at the walkway.

Realizing that he had no other choice, Eli wiped another tear from his eyes, turned his car on, and drove away for the place that caused him so much pain.

***

As Eli drove to the walkway, the downpour turned into a light drizzle.

When he pulled into the parking lot of the walkway, Eli's headlights pointed at Christian, who was standing beside his blue Nissan truck.

Even when Eli felt so low, he couldn't help but notice how attractive Christian was.

Eli parked next to Christian, turned off the headlights and got out of his car.

When he exited the car, he could smell the hard rain that just took place. The air was degrees cooler. And everything around him seemed calm.

But there was a storm inside Eli that wouldn't ease up.

Eli looked up at Christian, who was smiling. But when Christian noticed Eli's frown, his red puffy eyes, and his runny nose, his smile faded.

"Damn," Christian said, picking himself off of his truck, "Whatever happened really did a number on you."

"Am I really that hideous?" Eli asked.

"Nah," Christian said, wrapping his arm around Eli's shoulder and leading them to the picnic table area. "But I can certainly tell that something is bothering you."

Christian set Eli down at one end of the table, and then sat down at the other end.

"Okay," Christian said, "spill it."

Eli told him the whole story. He included every detail; the moment the horrible family walked in the door to the very last moment when Eli slipped outside. He didn't cry, but talking about it made him relive the moments again, something that he wouldn't wish on his worst enemy.

When Eli finished the story, he looked at Christian, who had a grim look on his face. He had even managed to bum out the person who always seemed to have a positive outlook.

"Wow, that's rough. I'm so sorry that happened to you. Some people are just downright hateful. Hence the reason I tend to be a little antisocial."

Eli put his head on the wooden table. "I've dealt with some crazy stuff in the four years I have worked there, but this one takes the cake."

"Don't let them get to you," Christian said, which prompted Eli to lift his head and look at the man. "By letting them ruin your night, they are getting what they want. You need to prove them wrong, and go back to work next week and act like nothing ever happened."

"I don't know if I could ever show my face back at work," Eli said.

Christian sat there for a minute, unsure what to say. "It'll take time, but you'll be able to go back, and you'll keep doing your job the way you have always known how to do it."

Eli could feel his heart melting inside. How is it that this man could make him feel good inside, despite how bad he was feeling for himself. It felt like even though he was losing, he was winning.

Because he was near Christian.

Christian looked at Eli to make sure he was listening. "Look on the bright side; this is why you are going to school, so you don't have to deal with jackasses like them."

"You do have a point there," Eli said, breaking a smile.

"Uh oh," Christian yelled, pointing at Eli. "I see you smiling! This means you aren't broken!"

Eli smiled even more. The man sure knew how to bring out the best in him.

If only he knew if he was able to do the same to Christian.

Christian stood up and stood next to Eli. "So here is what we're going to do. You're going to stand up," he motioned for Eli to stand, "You're going to say 'screw them' then we are going to hug it out, and then you are going to promise me that you will go hiking with me tomorrow."

"Hiking?"

"Yeah. You need to get your mind off of what has happened. And I know you'll just sit at home tomorrow and feel sorry for yourself. So instead, you are going to go hiking with me and have some fun."

Eli smiled at Christian, "I thought you said that it was too cold to go hiking."

Christian folded his arms, realizing that Eli had him there. "True, but I'm sure it'll be nice out tomorrow. And if not, then we can keep each other warm." He started laughing at his own joke.

Don't tempt me, Eli thought.

"I'm good with that," Eli said.

"Good, now stand up."

Eli obeyed, standing up in front of Christian.

"Now, say 'screw them.'"

Eli wasn't sure how this was going to help anything, but he did it anyways. "Screw them."

"Louder."

Eli raised his voice. "Screw them."

Christian held his hand up to his ear, mocking Eli. "I can't hear you! Scream it!"

"SCREW THEM," Eli yelled.

"There ya go," Christian said, clapping his hands at Eli. Then he held his arms open wide. "Now, we hug it out."

Eli did what Christian said. He opened his arms and the two of them embraced in a hug.

So many feelings and senses embraced Eli all at once. Eli could smell the scent off of Christian, which gave Eli a sense of euphoria. Feeling Christian's arms around him felt so good. He also felt numb; he could no longer feel the pain that resulted from tonight. All he could feel was the warmth that was radiating from the man's spirit.

Then Eli realized something.

I'm falling for him.

That feeling overwhelmed him. He had never felt something like that before. Yes, he had had crushes on people in the past, but this feeling felt more than he could ever imagine.

Was this love?

Eli tried not to think about it. He didn't want to feel anything towards somebody who couldn't reciprocate the same.

But that was what confused Eli. Eli couldn't tell if Christian shared the same feelings. And he wasn't about to ask Christian if he did. He was afraid of what the answer would be.

The two men broke their hug, which felt longer than a few seconds to Eli.

"Now, don't get all mushy on me," Christian said, joking. "Before you know it, you'll be trying to kiss me."

Would that be such a bad thing?

The two started walking back to their vehicles.

"I wanna say thanks," Eli said after several moments of silence.

"For what?" Christian questioned.

"For this," he responded, indicating where they stood. "For making me feel better. Because you're right, I would have had a pity party for myself."

"That's what I'm here for," Christian said, giving one of his famous smiles that showed off his beautiful teeth.

Hopefully he'll be here for me for a long time.

"Don't forget," Christian said as Eli started walking to his car, "we are doing hiking tomorrow."

"You bet," Eli said, "I wouldn't miss it for the world."

Eli got in the car and buckled up. He hadn't hiked in years, nor did he really enjoy the experience. But the idea of being with Christian made it seem like a good idea.

Eli turned his car on, as well as the headlights. He put the car in reverse and started heading out of the parking lot, waving at Christian as he pulled past the blue Nissan truck.

Chapter Seven

Like Christian said it would be, the next day was gorgeous. It always seemed to be beautiful after a storm.

Eli woke up early that morning and got ready for the hike.

He wasn't sure about the temperature for that day, so he decided to play it safe and put on a long sleeve flannel shirt, and pants. Then he put on boots that he almost never wore. When he slipped them on, he could feel his feet tightening from the lack of room. But he was determined not to slip and fall, looking like an idiot in front of Christian.

After meeting and talking with Christian the night before, Eli felt mentally numb. For him, that was a good thing. It was a lot better than the alternative, which was to replay the prior night's scene at work, which only brought up angry and hurtful feelings.

When Eli returned home that night, he told his parents what had happened. They tried to act sympathetic at first, for his sake. But eventually, they couldn't help but tell him how silly it was to get all worked up over what happened at a job that wasn't anywhere related to his career. Eli knew what they said was true, but he couldn't help but take it personally, since he strived so hard to be the best at everything he worked at.

He was going to make sure that what happened was not going to affect his day.

Once he was fully ready to go, he grabbed his phone and checked for messages. He had messaged Christian prior to getting ready to see where they wanted to meet.

Christian had responded with: **Let's meet at my place.**

Eli started feeling anxious. He was going to meet Christian at his home? Did that mean that Christian was starting to feel the same way that Eli felt about him?

Stupid, he said about himself, *people who are friends do meet at each other's houses.*

Eli texted Christian for the address and headed downstairs.

"Well now," Diane said as she walked towards the kitchen and noticed Eli walking down the stairs, "What are you doing up? I figured you would still be stewing in self-pity over what occurred last night."

Eli made a face at her, and said, "Thanks for putting salt on the wound, mother." He always called her mother when he was irritated with her. Then he said, "I had a friend invite me for a hike. He said it would get my mind off of what happened last night."

That caught his mother's attention. "Who is this friend of yours? You never mention hanging out with friends, except for Tori, who you claim you aren't dating."

Could Eli detect suspicion in his mother's voice? Did she suspect something?

"Christian is a friend from school. He is in one of my history classes. He's pretty cool."

Technically, Eli wasn't lying. Christian did go to the same school as Eli did. And as far as Eli knew, he might have also taken a history class there.

That seemed to have satisfied his mother, for now. "Well I'm glad you're getting out of this house for a change. Don't be late for supper though. I'm making meatloaf."

Eli felt relieved to know that he was now off the hook. He edged towards the back door, grabbing a spare pair of shoes for when he got done with the hike. "I wouldn't miss it for the world," he told his mother as he walked out the door.

***

Eli followed the directions his GPS gave him to get to Christian's house. So far, he had driven all the way across town, and was now on a two lane road in the Cyprus Valley community, a part of town that he rarely visited.

"Your destination is on the right," announced Judy, Eli's nickname for the GPS who gave him directions.

Eli took the next right, which was a driveway that went slightly up a hill. At the top of the hill was a moderate-sized home that was planted in front of a steep forest. When Eli pulled up in front of the house, he noticed that Christian had worked hard to keep the place looking nice. The grass was nicely manicured, with not one stray strand sticking up. Flowers were planted along the edge of the house, a combination of reds, yellows, and purples all mixed up, barely visible in their young blooms.

Eli got out of the car, noticing the sound of a meowing cat. His eyes looked towards the ground to see a spotted calico cat, not sure how to respond to the trespasser on its land.

"Hi there, pretty kitty," Eli said. He was always fond of the furry creatures. In fact, he had a gray and brown tabby cat named Zane, who he had to look forward to seeing when he returned home from today's adventure.

Eli reached down to pet the cat. It was hesitant at first, but once it got used to Eli's scent, the cat embraced him, and eventually rolled onto its back so Eli could rub its belly.

"Don't let Yoda get used to you, or he'll never let you leave."

Eli looked towards the porch and found Christian coming down the steps. He was all dressed for the hike as well. He looked way more prepared for what was ahead than Eli. But Eli had admitted from the beginning that he hadn't done it in years, so there wouldn't be any jokes coming from Christian.

"Yoda," Eli asked, continuing to rub the cat. "That's a clever name."

"Love it, you do," said Christian, mocking the infamous *Star Wars* character.

"Lucky for you," Eli started, rising to an upright position, leaving Yoda on his back, begging for more attention, "I'm a huge Star Wars fan. Otherwise, I would be making so much fun of you for the name that you cursed your cat with."

Christian chuckled. "Now that you're inadvertently making fun of me, are you ready to go hiking?"

"I thought you'd never ask."

The two left the cat where he was. Yoda didn't bother to get up and follow them.

Christian led Eli to a homemade trail that wasn't far from his home. Eli was sure glad that they were walking up a trail, instead of the leaves and sticks that he had imagined they would be walking on.

"Did you make this?" Eli asked.

"Yeah," responded Christian. "Once my parents split, and my mom moved down to Georgia, I got the house that she had been living in. I was living with my dad at the time, so there was no way up this mountain until I decided that I wanted to clear a path. It took a long time, but I think it turned out great."

"I'd say," said Eli. "I'm so glad I'm walking on this instead of the snake pits."

"You don't like snakes?"

Eli shook his head negatively. "Let's just say that if I was to see a snake on this trip, you would have to carry me, because I would fall over dead in an instant."

"I wouldn't mind doing that," Christian said, then let out a huge laugh.

Is he flirting with me, or is he playing one of those "no homo" jokes that are never funny?

"So I've been thinking," Eli said, trying to force the thought of Christian flirting with him out of his head.

"Uh huh," said Christian, continuing to climb up the mountain.

"Well, you paid for dinner a couple of weeks ago, so it's only fair that I take you out for lunch or dinner sometime."

"No, you don't have to," Christian said. "I wanted to do that."

"And I want to do this," Eli responded back. "So come on, when are you free?"

Christian kept walking upwards, thinking in his head when he was available. Then he responded, "Well, I won't really be free until next weekend. But, what if we had lunch sometime on campus?"

Eli liked that idea. "That sounds great to me."

For a while, the two of them hiked up the mountain in silence. Eli was unsure of what to say to the man in front of him. He didn't want to bring up the usual small talk that he usually brought up.

Nor did he want to bombard Christian with questions about his sexuality. So instead, he decided to have a little fun with the hiking expert.

Eli started walking faster, which resulted in him edging closer to Christian, who had been walking in front of Eli the entire trip.

"I was wondering if you would be able to make it up here with me," Christian teased.

"You forget, sir that I walk from end to end of *Arcade Hut* a million times per shift. I can pretty much walk any distance or incline when I want to."

"So why are you just now able to catch up to me?" Christian asked.

"I was enjoying the scenic view," Eli responded, taking a chance at being flirtatious.

It seemed to have worked. Christian worked hard to keep a smile from reaching his face, but eventually failed, who had a smile from ear to ear.

Just when Eli thought that they would never reach the end of the trail, they reached a clearing that showed a view of Pinecrest. The view took Eli's breath away.

"Now I know where you go when I can't get a hold of you," Eli joked. "This is incredible."

"It is," Christian agreed.

The two stood there for what seemed like forever. The view was beautiful, but it wasn't what Eli was focusing on. He kept thinking that this was Christian's hideout, his sanctuary. And he let Eli visit it. It made Eli feel special, but at the same time, it confused him.

Does he feel something for me too?

Eli didn't dare speak. He would stand next to Christian until the man decided it was time to go back down. Christian radiated peace and calmness, which was allowing Eli to be the same way.

Is there a chance I could feel this way forever?

Christian broke out of his trance and gave Eli his attention again. "Sorry for ignoring you. I could stay up here forever. Ready to go?"

"Only if you are," Eli said.

They started walking back down the trail together. Christian was much more talkative on the way down. He asked Eli questions about his degree, his family, and what he wanted to do after graduation. Eli was glad that he was asking the questions for a change.

By the time they reached the bottom of the trail, Eli was exhausted. Afraid of being embarrassed in front of Christian, Eli didn't take many deep breaths, unless there was enough distance between the two of them. Even though he thought he stayed fit by keeping active with his daily activities, he was sure that he would be sore in the morning.

Christian started walking in a different direction from Eli, so he could meet Yoda, who was crawling back over to the driveway when he heard his master return from his hike.

"Do you wanna come in?" Christian asked Eli as Yoda began to lie on his back so Christian could rub his belly.

It was a tempting offer to Eli. But he thought against it, afraid that if he went in Christian's home, he would become more attached to the man than he already was, if that was even possible.

If they continued to stay friends, he knew that an opportunity would come up where he would be able to come to Christian's home again.

"That's okay," Eli said, "I have some homework I need to take care of. And I'm sure you might have some too."

"You're right," Christian said. "I've been putting it off for long enough."

Eli walked over to where Christian and Yoda were, and rubbed the cat goodbye. Then he looked at Christian, "Don't forget, I'm taking you to lunch the first chance we get."

"I'm holding you to it," Christian responded.

They shook hands, like they always did before parting ways. Eli knew he was getting ahead of himself, but the handshakes felt like they were more from two lovers than two friends. Eli was once again reminded that he was falling for the man, hard. And the idea that Christian didn't feel the same way about him was heartbreaking.

As Christian picked up Yoda and starting walking into his house, Eli starting walking towards his car. He only hoped that this wouldn't be the last time he was there.

Chapter Eight

The cold came back as soon as it left. Eli tried as best as he could to stay warm, despite the fact that he only had on a light jacket. He had no idea that the weather would turn so violent so fast.

It had been three days since his hike with Christian. And yes, Eli was indeed sore after the journey up the mountain. But it was all worth it to Eli.

It had become apparent to him that Christian was his second source for life. He was amazed how fast he had fallen for the man. And he had done so without learning details of Christian's intimate side, nor acting on his own intimate side. Just feeling Christian's presence gave Eli a new look on life. And he was already unable to foresee himself going down a road where Christian wasn't there with him.

The urge to see if Christian was at the point where he wanted to date was overwhelming Eli. He promised himself that he wouldn't be forward with Christian, nor would he try to pry into the man's private life. But the thought of the man he had feeling for having feelings for someone else, or even not sharing the same feelings for Eli, seemed unbearable.

Eli kept telling himself that he needed to push those thoughts out of his mind and wait for Christian to be honest with him. But he knew that the two of them would have to face this issue head-on, and he was unsure what the results would be.

Today was the day that Eli and Christian finally decided to

meet up at school for lunch. Eli had just gotten out of his last class of the morning, and raced to the center of campus to the place where they agreed to eat.

"What's *McAllister's*?" Christian had asked over the phone the night before.

"It's a deli on campus. I just discovered it a few weeks ago, and I'm in love with it. I'm pretty sure that you'll enjoy it too."

"You're sure you don't want to eat off campus?" Christian asked. It appeared that he wasn't settled on the idea of eating somewhere he was unfamiliar with.

"It wouldn't bother me," Eli said, "But I have class at 1:30. I don't wanna have to rush."

"I can understand that," Christian said sympathetically. "Okay, I'm in."

They had agreed to meet at noon. So Eli hoped that he wasn't too late.

When Eli made it to the front door and sat at a table nearby, he pulled out his phone and started messaging Christian.

I'm here. What's your location?

He hoped that Christian responded soon. He didn't want to have to rush his lunch with the man so he could make it to class on time.

Eli's phone vibrated on the table in front of him.

Just got out of class. I'll be there as soon as I can.

So Eli sat there, waiting for Christian to arrive.

As he waited, he noticed that the line inside McAllister's was getting longer. But he decided not to get in line in case the line went faster than Christian could walk.

Eli was beginning to think that he was going to freeze to death, and debated going inside, when he saw Christian's figure heading in his direction.

Thank God!

Christian was much more prepared for the cold weather than Eli was. He was fully buttoned up, with a scarf and toboggan. To some, Christian's attire may have seemed over the top, but Eli would have killed to have dressed that smart.

"I hope you have another jacket," Christian said as he walked near Eli and pointed at the jacket that Eli was wearing, "Because I don't think this one is going to do it for you."

"You're telling me," Eli responded.

"You look frozen," Christian said with a smile.

"That's because I am."

"Wimp," Christian joked.

"Says the person that is wearing the thicker coat," Eli shot back.

"Touché," Christian admitted.

Eli went for the door into McAllister's and held it open for Christian. "Ready?"

"You bet, I'm starved."

As the two walked in, Christian immediately had to take off his coat and toboggan because of the heat inside. While Christian's hair was flattened because of his hat, he still looked hot in Eli's eyes. But it did remind him of how Christian wore his hair back in high school. Could he even see small flecks of gray in the man's hair?

Eli found it comfortable inside and kept this jacket on. They walked up to the last person in line and waited for their turn to order.

"It's a good thing we hiked before the weather turned bad again," Eli said.

"Yeah, I'm glad we got to do it," Christian responded. "Are you okay from last Saturday's incident?"

It took Eli a second to realize what the man was asking, and then remembered the hateful customers. "Oh yeah, hanging out with you helped with that."

"Have you gone back to work?"

"Not yet, because I don't work on weekdays. But I hope that when I go back, things will be okay again."

"I hope so too," Christian said.

They spent their time in the long line talking about how their day had gone so far, and what classes they had taken and what they had left for the day. During that time, Eli found out that Christian was taking a lot of math classes as his minor.

"Math? I couldn't imagine taking it at a university level."

Christian shrugged his shoulders. "It's not that bad. I actually enjoy it sometimes. And the teachers here are great. But it's definitely not the classes like we took in high school.

Eli was instantly reminded of the boy across the aisle from him so many years ago, and compared him to the man that stood before him today. He had changed so much. They both had.

"Next, please," said the cashier in front of them. She had to raise her voice to catch their attention.

"Oops," Eli said. They walked to the cashier to order their food.

"What would you recommend?" Christian asked, unsure of the new menu in front of him.

Eli looked at the menu with him. "Well, everything on here is great. But personally, I'm a fan of the pot roast sandwich right now."

"That sounds good," Christian said, having made up his mind. "I'll have that."

"Two of those," Eli said before the cashier could turn away.

Before Christian could reach for his wallet, Eli handed the cashier his credit card. "I told you," he said, "This is my treat."

Christian didn't question it much further, and stopped his hand from reaching his back pocket.

They received their drinks and ticket, and walked over to a table.

"I had no idea they served hot food here," Christian said. "When you said deli, I figured it was all cold."

"I thought the same thing," Eli responded. "But like sushi, it was not what I expected it to be."

Christian chuckled, and then took a sip from his drink.

What do I say now? Eli thought to himself.

"Uh," he started out, "How are *things*?"

"Things?"

"Yeah, the thing that reacquainted us."

"Oh," Christian said, realizing what Eli was referring to and realized that Eli was trying to be discreet. "It's alright, been chatting on the forum. And then I've been chatting with you."

"Have you been on any dates?" Eli asked, regretting it as soon as he asked it.

Christian laughed it off. "No. Haven't done that yet."

"What about your parents? Have you thought about telling them?"

"No," Christian responded very suddenly. Then he said, "Well, you know the story with my dad and step-mom. As for my mom and step-dad, I haven't told them either, and they're too far away for it to matter, I think."

Eli realized that Christian had brought up about his mother moving away several times, but he didn't know much more about that side of Christian's family. "Where did your mom move to?"

"Savannah, Georgia. She moved there once the divorce was final."

"Oh," Eli said with a sad tone. "I'm sorry."

"It's okay," Christian said. "She enjoys it down there. And she loves my step-dad. I don't get to see them much, but when I do, I enjoy being with them. They're actually coming up this weekend. That's why I can't take you to a movie."

"A movie?" Eli had no idea what he was talking about.

The two looked at each other, not sure what the other was saying. Then it struck Christian.

"Whoa, I'm sorry. I completely forgot I never asked you. I had wanted to ask if you wanted to go see a movie with me. But then my mom called and asked if she could come and stay with me."

Eli was excited by the thought that Christian wanted to spend more time with him, but was quickly saddened that it wasn't going to happen. But the thought that Christian had wanted to ask him made him feel special.

"You're fine," Eli said, waving off Christian's apology. "Yeah, it would have been nice to have gone to a movie with you, but you deserve some time with your family."

Christian smiled. "Thanks for understanding."

"No problem," Eli responded. "But now that I think about it, what movie were you hoping to go see, if I may ask?"

"I don't wanna say," Christian said, suddenly acting reserved.

"Why not?" Eli questioned.

"Because you'll laugh at me."

Eli had no idea what would make Christian so insecure about himself. "I'm sure I would enjoy it. Come on and tell me."

Christian sat there for a moment and contemplated telling Eli. After a few moments, he said it. "I was thinking about going to see *Frozen*."

Eli was not expecting that answer. Yes, he was a fan of Disney when he was younger and even indulged himself in a Disney classic every once in awhile. But what surprised him was that a macho man like Christian was suggesting that he and another man go see it together. Eli now understood why Christian didn't want to tell him.

"Go ahead," Christian said, "Give your judgment."

Eli took a long sip from his drink, and then said, "While it wasn't the first thing I thought you were going to say, it's not a bad choice. I am a fan of Disney, and I've heard that it was a good movie." Eli wanted to say more, wanted Christian to know that he didn't think the idea was stupid. Eli wanted to plan as many occasions with Christian as possible. "I think we should go see it after your family leaves."

Eli's response raised Christian's spirits. It was clear that Christian had feared being made fun of. Once again, Eli noticed the person he had seen storm out of the school so many years ago.

"Great! I'm really excited about it!"

"Me too," Eli replied.

A couple of minutes passed before Eli checked the time on his phone. Only thirty-five minutes before Eli had to report to class.

Eli leaned over the table so nobody would be able to hear what he was about to tell Christian. "It usually never takes this long for me to get my food."

"I was wondering the same thing," Christian added.

Finally, a waitress came by with a duplicate order of food on a tray.

"I am so sorry about the wait. I couldn't find where you guys were." She smiled and took the ticket back up to the front.

"Let's hurry and start eating before she changes her mind," Eli joked.

Christian laughed and acted on Eli's comment. Eli watched Christian take his first bite, wondering what his reaction would be about the deli that Eli had talked him into going to.

Eli noticed a nod of approval before Christian said, "Pretty dang good."

They both ate in silence. Eli wasn't sure why Christian wasn't speaking, but Eli wasn't speaking because he wanted to hurry and eat so he didn't have to rush his time with Christian.

Once their plates were clean, Christian wiped his mouth with a napkin and put his jacket back on. "That was really good."

"I'm glad you approve," Eli said. "We need to make this a usual thing."

"Definitely."

They walked outside and braced for the cold weather ahead. It didn't seem to have affected Christian with his extra layer of clothing, but for Eli, it felt as if a block of ice had hit his chest. He imagined a fire surrounding him so he could embrace the cold.

"Where are you headed to next?" Christian asked.

"I'm heading to the Brown building," Eli said, trying not to bring attention to his chattering teeth.

"Great, I'm in Darden," Christian said, starting to head in the direction in front of them. "We're right next to each other."

As they started walking, snow flurries started to dance around them. Christian teased Eli, saying that he was making it snow because he wanted to watch *Frozen* so badly.

That may be true, but not because of the snow.

Eli rammed his shoulder into Christian's arm because of the comment, laughing when it took Christian by surprise. That resulted in a shoulder being rammed into Eli's arm.

The two climbed the stairs that took them to the main levels of the Brown and Darden buildings. Eli didn't want to depart from Christian, but his need to be in class a little early overcame him. He didn't know why he still had to be early for everything, even during his last semester in college.

"Well, I really enjoyed myself," Eli said, slowing stepping to the left where his building was located.

"Indeed it was. Thanks again for treating me to lunch."

"It was my pleasure. Now, *you* have to pay if you want me to go see *Frozen*."

They laughed, following with Christian saying, "That's up for debate."

"We'll see," Eli said.

Christian held his hand out. "Until next time."

Eli shook the man's hand, already planning in his head when

that time would be.

Chapter Nine

The weekend had come and gone. Christian's family had come into town, which meant that Eli had not heard from the man in days. Not speaking to Christian gave Eli an uneasy feeling, like he was missing something important in his life.

It was Tuesday before Eli heard from him.

"Long time, no talk," Christian said after Eli answered the phone.

"Indeed it has," Eli agreed. "I was starting to think that you had disappeared on me."

"Not on your life," Christian chuckled.

Eli asked Christian how the weekend with his parents went. Christian said it went really well. His mom cooked them a big spread, which was something Christian missed a lot about his mother living hours away. His step-father helped fix something in Christian's Nissan that caused something inside the truck to rattle. Eli didn't understand anything he was saying while he was talking technical, mechanical babble.

"Overall, it sounds like a good weekend," Eli responded.

"Yeah, it was." Christian then paused. "The reason I'm calling is to see if you were still up to go with me to see *Frozen*. I checked the theatre, and it's still playing."

The man really wants to see this movie.

Luckily for Eli, he'd go see anything as long as he got to be with Christian.

"I'd love to go," Eli said before Christian could change his mind.

"Great," Christian said ecstatically. Eli could hear his smile from across the phone. "I'm free tomorrow. Will that work for you?"

It didn't take Eli long to find an answer. "That sounds good to me."

"Wonderful," Christian said.

***

Eli had it all figured out.

He'd go to school and be back just in time to catch the four o'clock showing with Christian.

He was actually looking forward to seeing the movie. He knew that anything could happen in a movie theatre. And if nothing did happen, at least he got to spend the afternoon with the man he had a crush on.

Eli went downstairs to a quiet house the morning of the planned trip to the movie. His sisters had already gone off to school, and his father had already departed for work. However, Eli did hear a sound coming from inside his parent's bedroom.

Diane was getting ready in the master bathroom, putting her graying, brunette hair into a bun.

"Good morning, mom," Eli said, slinging his backpack over his shoulder. "I'm gone."

She looked at Eli and leaned in for a kiss on the cheek.

"Bye bye, baby," she said as he kissed her.

He turned around and started walking out of the room.

"Oh, wait!" Diane spoke up, trying to catch Eli's attention before he left.

Eli leaned back into the bathroom. "Yeah?"

"Can you pick up your sister this afternoon?"

"Sure," Eli responded. "I'll pick her up on my way back from school and then I'll drop her off."

"Well," his mom started, "I'll need you to stay with her. I have to take your grandfather to the doctor, and I don't know when I'll be back."

Eli's heart felt like it had stopped beating.

But I'm supposed to meet Christian today.

"Can't Carrie pick her up for me and watch her?" Eli asked. "She'll be in town anyways."

"Carrie has to work," his mother replied.

Eli couldn't help but show his disappointment.

"What?" his mother asked, noticing her son's change in posture. "Did you have somewhere you have to be?"

Eli thought about it and weighed his options. Should he tell his mother that he wanted to go see a movie with another man, the same man that he started hanging out with out of the blue, or should he wait and see if he could get to the movie without having to tell her?

Once again, he wished that he didn't have to hide who he was.

No, he didn't have to hide. He chose to hide.

Eli finally decided that he would take his chances and wait and see how the day played out.

"No," Eli responded. Then it occurred to him that he could put his excuse on his back and forth arguments with his sister. "I just thought that Carrie could pick up Ruth for a change."

His mother gave him a look. "Don't be too hard on your sister."

"Okay," Eli sighed.

He waved his mother goodbye and walked out of the room.

***

Towards the end of the day at school, Eli had not heard from either Christian nor his mother. Christian hadn't messaged him because he was expecting to meet Eli later that day. And his mother hadn't contacted him because her plans hadn't changed as of that moment.

As he headed to his car at the edge of campus, he decided to text Christian with the bad news. He didn't want to stand him up.

I'm not able to go to the movies this afternoon.

He was in the car and turned it on when Christian responded.

Why? :(

Eli didn't understand why his heart fluttered whenever he received a message from Christian that had an emoticon in it. It broke his heart to see that this one was a sad face. Was Christian really sad because Eli bailed on their outing together?

I have to pick up my sister and watch her. The movie will already be starting by the time my mom gets home. I'm sorry.

Eli started driving out of the school's parking lot. He had wanted to go and be with Christian so badly. And who knew the next time Eli would have an opportunity to be near Christian again.

Eli's phone vibrated in his cup holder. Eli picked it up and diverted enough attention from the road to read what it said.

I understand. Things happen. I was really looking forward to going, though.

You and I both, Eli responded.

***

"Hi, Eli," Ruth said as she got in the car from the car riders section at school. "How was your day?"

"Fine," Eli said, shortly. He knew that it wasn't his sister's fault that he couldn't go to the movies. He just wished that he could have been at the movies with Christian.

"How was your day?" Eli then asked, trying to show that he wasn't mad at her.

His sister started talking about her day in the seventh grade, talking about all of the petty things that Eli had once been consumed with. He tried to pay attention to her, but it was so hard for him. Especially when he was fantasizing where he could be at that moment instead of where he was.

When Eli pulled into the driveway, he was shocked to see his mother sweeping out the garage. He thought that she was going to be late.

Realizing this set anger into Eli's bones. He could have went to the movies.

He got out of the car and walked over to his mother. "Mom," he said, "I thought you said that you were going to be late."

His mother didn't detect any anger in his voice. She looked at him from sweeping and said, "Your grandfather's appointment went quicker than I thought it would be. I figured that since you were already planning to pick up your sister that it wouldn't matter if you could already do it."

Eli tried really hard to not show his irritation. If his mother had messaged him and said that she would be able to pick up Ruth, then everything would have went according to plan. And Eli would have been able to see Christian.

Now that wasn't going to happen.

Or could it? Eli wasn't sure of the time. There could still be a chance that Eli could tell Christian that things were back on and be at the theatre before the movie ever began.

He ran inside and checked the time on the stove.

4:05 p.m.

Eli's heart sank. There was no way that he, nor Christian, would be able to make it there without missing a major chunk of the movie.

There's always next time.

That was true, but Eli couldn't help but think that his time with Christian was more limited than he realized.

Chapter Ten

The weekend was arriving quicker than Eli realized. It seemed like every day was getting shorter and shorter, when in reality, they were getting longer and longer. Eli was starting to believe that it was because he wasn't near Christian.

Eli had tried to reschedule to go to the movies with Christian after Eli had to bail on him. But unfortunately, Christian said that his schedule was full until the weekend. So Eli had to wait. But he had high hopes of being able to make it up to Christian, by asking him to go to see *Frozen* once the weekend arrived.

Friday afternoon approached, and Eli checked the theatre's website to see if *Frozen* still appeared on their showing list. At the very bottom of the theatre's website, Eli discovered that the movie was still playing there, but the show times were very limited. That could only mean that the movie was to exit soon.

He had to go see it with Christian.

He picked up his phone and started messaging Christian. **Frozen is still in theatres. Do you wanna go see it tonight?**

Eli had a smile on his face. He had plans on making it up to Christian for missing out on Wednesday's outing.

Several hours had passed, and Eli had not heard anything from Christian. Christian's responses were usually delayed, but it never took him this long to reply.

***

It was Monday, and Eli still had not heard from Christian. The temptation to try and message him again was growing, but he decided against it. He knew that if and when Christian finally checked his phone, he would notice that Eli had messaged him multiple times.

But what if Christian had already read his messages, and he was choosing to ignore them? Maybe Christian had had enough of talking to him.

Eli tried not to think about that. He thought that he and Christian had grown close over the past couple of months. Surely Christian wouldn't drop him at the top of a hat.

It was several hours into the afternoon when Eli felt his phone vibrating in his pocket. He pulled it out and was amazed at who it was.

Christian!

Hey there.

Was that all that he could say to Eli after going AWOL for three days?

Hi, Eli responded. **I was beginning to think that you fell off of the face of the earth.**

Christian responded, **Nah, I just had a friend over for the weekend and didn't look at my phone the entire time.**

It was a relief to Eli to know that Christian hadn't decided to ignore him. But he couldn't help but wonder what kind a friend, especially a friend that Eli had never heard of, would cause someone to ignore their phone all weekend.

A friend with benefits, Eli thought to himself.

No, Eli quickly said to himself. *Just because he didn't tell you about his friend, doesn't mean that they are lovers.*

Eli wanted to know more about this *friend*, but knew that

questioning Christian about it would make Christian think that Eli didn't believe him. So all he said was: **I'm glad you had fun. And I'm even happier that you have returned to society.**

Although Eli's message was friendly, his thoughts were different. He had no idea if Christian was telling him the truth. But what he did know was that he felt jealousy coursing through his veins, and he didn't like the feeling. Was it because Christian had never invited him to stay over, or was it the fact that Christian didn't tell him that he was having a friend over?

He sounded like a jealous boyfriend.

But why did any of that matter? If Christian had one day asked Eli to spend the weekend with him, Eli would have said no because his parents would be suspicious of a 22-year old spending the night with somebody. And even if he had said yes, there would have been something that would come up, which would result in Eli bailing on his plans. And Christian wasn't Eli's boyfriend, so what gave Eli the right to know every single thing that Christian did?

What got to Eli was the fact that Christian had said that he wasn't ready to date. What if he wasn't interested in Eli, but he was interested in this other person? No, Eli couldn't think that. The thought of caring for someone, maybe even *loving* someone, and that someone not feeling the same way about him, seemed almost unbearable.

Yeah, it's good to be back, Christian responded.

So what did you both do over the weekend?

Well we hiked. Other than that, we just laid around, Christian texted back.

That was not the response that Eli had wanted to hear. Lying around could be anything. And Eli's mind was starting to travel places that he didn't want it to go.

For the remainder of the day, it was as if Christian had never left. They spent the day catching up and talking about the new things that had happened in their lives since they last talked. Eli was glad that things were starting to get back to normal.

But he wasn't able to get the thought out of his head that Christian was starting to fall for someone else.

Chapter Eleven

Five days had passed since Christian's return on Eli's radar. Since Christian returned and started talking to Eli again, Eli was unable to stop thinking about him, and the *friend* that suddenly entered Christian's life. Christian never mentioned the weekend again, but it was in the back of Eli's mind, as if Christian was regularly throwing it in Eli's face.

As each day passed, Christian's messages to Eli became more and more infrequent. When he would finally respond, he would say that he was busy with things.

Eli didn't fully believe the man. Sure, Christian was a busy person, but he always fit time in to say a few words over a text message. Ever since his weekend with this new person in his life, things were just not the same anymore.

But Eli had hopes to change that.

He had decided that he had left Christian alone about "dates" and "boyfriends" for long enough. He was going to ask Christian out, and hopefully be able to take the next step with the man that he cared for.

It was only forty-five minutes until he had to report into work, so he had to act fast. He didn't want the opportunity to slip through his fingers.

He dialed Christian's number and waited for a response on the other end.

"Hello," Christian said.

Eli went straight to the point. "So I've been thinking."

When Christian realized who it was on the other end, he responded, "What have you been thinking about?"

Eli hesitated for a second. It was now or never, and he didn't want to never find out if there was a chance for the two of them. "I've been thinking that we should go out sometime."

There was no response on Christian's end of the phone, so Eli continued to speak. "The truth is, Christian, that I've had a crush on you for some time. You're not like any person I have ever encountered. You're intelligent, funny, you're in shape, and you've never asked me to send a photo of myself with my shirt off."

That did get a small chuckle out of Christian.

"I've been really happy since I have started talking to you," Eli said. "I think I have deep feelings for you, and I think that you have feelings for me too."

"Oh boy," Christian said. Couldn't he say more than that?

"I'm sorry that I'm dumping all of this on you at once," Eli continued, hoping that an apology would help the awkward situation that he had put himself in. "It's just that I have been keeping all of my feelings inside for some time. And I was beginning to think that you were starting to drift away. I thought that telling you would help for some reason."

It took a moment, but Eli finally heard Christian start to respond.

"Listen, Eli," Christian started, "I'm flattered that you think so highly of me. But to be honest, I really just want to be friends with you."

Eli could barely feel his heart shatter, he was so numb. A wave of sadness overcame him. And was that a tear that was starting to form in the corner of Eli's eye?

"Eli, are you there?" Christian asked after a few seconds.

Eli tried hard to regain himself before saying, "Yeah, I'm sorry. I'm here. And I understand that you just want to be friends."

A sigh of relief could be heard over the phone. "I'm so glad that you say that. Because I would hate to lose you as a friend."

"Me too," Eli said. Then something occurred to him and made him wonder. "Can I ask you a question?"

"Sure."

"Is there someone that you want to be more than friends with?"

"As a matter of fact, there is," Christian responded.

Now it felt as if someone was stomping on the broken pieces of Eli's heart. It was bad enough that he didn't want to be with Eli, but it was worse to know that he was interested in someone else.

"Oh?" Eli tried to contain his voice so it wouldn't get high pitched and squeaky. But he failed. "Who is it?"

"You wouldn't know him," Christian said. "He lives in Asheville. I met him over POF."

Eli could almost curse the match-making website. On one hand, it had provided the tool to meeting the man that was now beyond his reach. It provided him someone that gave him company, advice and made him happy. On the other hand, it provided someone the tools to also find Christian, and to spark something in Christian that Eli apparently wasn't able to do.

"I see," Eli said. "So, have you met him in person yet?"

Eli regretted asking Christian the question before the man even spoke. "Yes, I have," Christian said. "The first time we met, we went to a movie. I was so intimidated by his good looks that I got so nervous. I wanted to hold his hand so badly, but the fear crept up on me every time I reached out to grab his hand. When Jaden noticed me pulling back, he reached out and held mine. Then we held hands for the entire movie."

Jaden? It sure sounds like someone who would reach out and crush someone's heart and dreams.

Like mine.

Then Eli thought about the movie that the two men saw together. Did they go see *Frozen*, the same movie that Christian had asked Eli to go see? The thought of Eli's suspicions being true made him feel the utmost betrayal and jealousy towards Christian.

"Then he came over and spent the weekend over here," Christian continued. "I've spent so much time getting to know him, and then I realized that I had feelings for him."

Eli couldn't refrain from asking his next question. "Was that the time that you didn't respond for a whole weekend?"

"Uh, yeah," Christian said slowly.

Oh my God. Eli felt every cell in his body clench tight, as if he was fighting for every ounce of air available. If this wasn't a stroke, he didn't know what was.

"I know that we held hands," Christian continued without waiting for a response from Eli, "But I don't know how he feels about me. And I don't think my full feelings toward him are apparent. I want to ask him out, but I don't know how or when to do it."

Eli knew that he was acting selfish. Maybe he was even acting dramatic. But he couldn't help but clutch his chest from the lack of breath. It was as if all source of life had been ripped from him.

He knew that he had feelings for Christian; feelings that he had never felt before. But he had no idea that he had fallen so far for the man that the thought of not being with him felt fatal.

"Eli," Christian finally said, "Are you there?"

Eli felt a big tear roll down his face. He wiped it away quickly before it could hit the ground. *No,* Eli decided, *I'm not going to act devastated while he is on the phone.*

"I'm here," Eli said. "Listen, I have to head to work right now. So I'll talk to you later, okay?"

"Okay," Christian said. Eli thought that Christian had hung up his end of the line before Christian returned. "Eli, are you okay?"

"You bet," Eli said, trying to hide his disappointment. "I just really have to go."

"Okay, bye."

"Bye."

Eli looked at the clock and realized that he should have left for work earlier than he should have. He pushed Christian out of his mind for a second and ran down the stairs.

He could see his mother in the den paying bills as he came down the staircase. He didn't take the time to go into the office like he usually did.

"Bye, mom," he said, hurriedly. "I'm late for work." He didn't wait to hear her respond before he was out the door and on his way to the car.

He took a deep breath once he entered the vehicle. *Forget him. He obviously doesn't care about you. He never did. So why should you give him the satisfaction by crying over him?* Then his own thoughts conflicted him. *No, there was something there. I felt it. He may not want to admit it, but there has to be something between us.*

These thoughts raced through Eli's head the entire way to work. The urge hit him to remove Christian from his phone, so that he wouldn't be tempted to contact him again. Then another urge hit him to call Christian back and confess his undying love for him.

Undying love? Did Eli really love this man? Sure, he felt more for this person than he had felt for anyone else before, male or female. But it did seem silly to think that Eli could love someone when he had never held hands with Christian, never kissed him, never made love to him.

His thoughts were still racing when he parked his car in the parking lot of *Arcade Hut.* He didn't want to go in there without a plan of action on how to deal with the Christian situation. Should he admit defeat and walk away from what made him so happy, or should he fight for Christian and risk getting hurt even more?

***

Eli had made up his mind by the time he entered the building. He had decided that he was going fight for the man that he cared for, maybe even loved. He knew that his chances weren't good, but he had to take a chance. He didn't want to one day say that he missed an opportunity to be with a great guy.

Tori was in her office when he clocked in.

"Well," she started, acting pouty, "Do my eyes deceive me? Is that Eli Cooper I see in front of me? No, that can't be, because Eli doesn't talk to me anymore."

Eli hadn't realized until that moment that he had neglected Tori since spending more time with Christian.

His facial expressions matched his feelings when he told Tori, "I'm sorry." He walked closer to her as she flipped her long, dark hair in disgust. "I never meant to ignore you. With school, and getting to know my new "friend," I just haven't had a lot of time on my hands. Don't forget that you were the one that encouraged me to find someone to be in my life."

When Tori realized that Eli had her there, she said, "Well, I sure hope that you are getting some out of him."

Eli's face began to blush from embarrassment. He couldn't believe that the man Eli told Tori about, the man he had a crush on, was interested in someone else.

And he was about to tell Tori.

"Well—"

"You haven't slept with him?" Tori asked, her jaw dropping down as far as it would go.

"Try not even kissing him," Eli replied.

"What?!" Tori squealed, which prompted Eli to put a hand over her mouth so that the rest of the building couldn't hear her. When he was sure that she wasn't going to make any more noise, he removed his hand.

"So you mean to tell me," Tori said, calmer than she was before, "That you have spent months talking to this guy, and nothing has happened with him?" When Eli's silence gave her the answer she needed, she asked, "Why has nothing happened with him?"

Eli shrugged. "I didn't know the answer to that until today. Before, I thought it was my hesitancy to be close to someone because of my own confliction with my sexuality. But today, I found out that he has feelings for someone."

Hearing that instantly set Tori on Eli's defense. "The bastard."

"He's not a bastard, Tori—"

"He is if he has been leading you on this entire time."

Eli shook his head to disagree with her. "Really, it's not his fault." He waited a moment to see if he was going to get any disagreement from her. When he realized that she was waiting for an explanation, he continued. "He said from the beginning that he was only looking for friends, and maybe in the future, he may look for more. He never said that he was interested in me."

Tori looked at him rather intently. "He may not have said that he was interested in you, but that didn't stop you from being interested in him, right?"

"Yeah," Eli admitted.

"So why fall for someone that you knew you never could have?"

Eli thought about it for a moment. "I was beginning to think that he did have some sort of feelings for me."

"So you mean that he led you on?"

Eli shook his head. "I didn't say that."

Tori interrupted him before he could defend Christian. "I know you, Eli. You may be a little naïve in this area, but even you wouldn't pursue someone that you couldn't have. He must have been sending you signals that kept you interested."

Eli hadn't thought about it that way. "You may be right about that."

When Tori was satisfied with her victory, she said, "So that makes him a bastard."

Eli shook his head in agreement to make Tori happy.

After nothing was said after awhile, Tori said, "So what are you going to do about this?"

"Huh?"

Tori sighed. "You obviously care about this guy, whether he sent you the wrong signals or not. You have never been a person to quit easily. I think you should fight for him. Who knows, maybe he is telling you that he is interested in someone else to test you."

This thought perked Eli up. Yes, maybe Christian was just playing hard to get. Christian had certainly teased Eli in the past. Maybe he was doing it now.

"You know," Eli started, making his way towards Tori's office door. He didn't want to get in trouble for not being at his station. "I came in here saying that I was going to fight for him, whether it was the right or wrong thing to do. After talking with you, I *know* that it is the right thing to do."

Tori bowed her head. "You're welcome."

Eli smiled. "This is why you're my best friend."

***

Eli was scheduled in the back of the building, working the bounce houses. He was with Lisa, who also hated working in this section. It bored Eli easily and made him rethink about having kids. But today, being in the back had its perks. For one thing, he wouldn't be at risk of facing someone like the old woman and her family that he faced weeks ago. Second, he would be able to message Christian without being detected by the managers.

Eli grabbed the keys to the ticket machines and pulled the wagon of tickets behind him. "Lisa," he said, looking across the station, "I'm going to fill up the games while it's slow."

Lisa took a moment to look up from her own phone to look at Eli. Some people weren't as cautious with their phone as he was. "Sure, go ahead."

As soon as he rolled up to the first game, he pulled his phone out and messaged Christian.

Hey, Christian messaged back, **Are you okay? You sounded upset on the phone earlier.**

It was harder for Eli to hide is feelings, it seemed.

I'm fine, Eli responded. **The phone conversation was awkward though.**

Yeah, I'm sorry about that. I just felt that you needed to know that truth.

He didn't know what came over him, but Eli had a feeling that this was the perfect opportunity to come clean with Christian.

I understand, Eli started. **And now I need you to know the truth about something.**

It took Christian a moment to respond before he sent **The truth about what?**

This is it, Eli thought, *It's now or never.*

The truth is that I didn't just want to go on a date with you. I have deep feelings for you, and I have had them for awhile. When you said that you weren't ready to date, I thought that you weren't ready to date anybody. So it was shock when you told me that you liked someone.

He sent the message. He breathed with relief. It felt good to get it all out and in the open.

It took Christian a while to respond. Eli thought that either he had scared the man off, or Christian was contemplating what to say next.

Finally, after several minutes, and several arcade games now replenished with tickets, Christian responded to Eli.

Yeah, I figured that you had feelings for me.

Reading that message took Eli by surprised. Was he really that transparent?

You knew?

Yes, Christian replied. **It dawned on me when you asked me to the movie after you were unable to make it the first time. To be honest, it freaked me out.**

Eli wasn't expecting that from Christian. The man was being the most honest that he had ever been before.

Why did it freak you out?

At this point, Eli didn't care if people saw him with his phone out or not. Right now, all that mattered was finding out the truth. The truth that he had been waiting for so long to find out.

Because, Christian responded, **I thought we were becoming really good friends. It was a shock to me when I realized that you felt more towards me.**

I'm sorry that I confused you. I wanted to ask you out the minute that I found you on POF. But you made it very clear that you were new to all of this. I didn't want to pressure you, and I wanted to get to know you better. As we got closer, I knew there was more to us than just friendship. Based on your actions towards me, I thought that you felt the same way.

Eli's fingers cramped after typing the long message. Unaware of the time that had passed by, he turned around to examine the area surrounding him. Fortunately, the area was just as dead as it was before. Another perk of working in the back. Confident that the managers would not be interested in checking on him and his co-workers anytime soon, he made his way into the private party room that *Arcade Hut* reserved for special events and birthday parties. He wanted to give his conversation with Christian his full attention, no matter what the repercussions would be if it affected his job performance.

By the time he made it into the room, made sure that the door was closed and the lights off, Eli took his attention back to his phone.

Christian had responded, with a response that Eli was not looking forward to reading.

I'm sorry that I gave you that impression. It was certainly not my intention.

I understand, Eli responded, **But at the same time, maybe you acted this way because you sub-consciously have feelings towards me.**

It didn't take Christian long to respond. **How could I have feelings towards you? I told you that I like someone else.**

Eli took a chance and responded with: **But you don't know if this guy likes you. You know that I like you. Why not see what could happen between us?**

As soon as Eli sent the message, he knew that he either brought the two of them closer together, or pushed them father apart.

It took Christian so long to respond, Eli went back out onto the work floor and resumed his task of filling games with tickets. Eli almost dropped everything when he felt his phone vibrate in his pants pocket.

Eli was so shocked when he read Christian's message.

Can we meet tonight? At the walkway?

Did it work? Was Eli able to convince Christian to abandon a chance with this guy, and instead pursue a relationship with him?

Assuming that Eli was correct, he was very fast to respond, before Christian could change his mind.

You bet.

Eli slid his phone back in his pocket and merrily returned to his work. He couldn't help but have a smile on his face. It looked as if he was about to get everything he had always wanted.

***

As soon as he was told that he could go home from work, Eli hurriedly clocked out and ran to his car. Eli checked his phone and saw that there was no message from Christian. That made him happy. That meant that Christian had not changed his mind to meet him tonight.

Which means that he hasn't changed his mind about us.

It only took him minutes to drive to the walkway. He risked a ticket by going faster than he should have. He was so eager to see Christian, the man who had made him so happy over the past few months, and hopefully for the months to come.

In the small amount of time that it took him to drive from *Arcade Hut* to the walkway, Eli came to a startling realization.

Eli, he is the one, *Eli thought. Nobody has made you feel as good about yourself like he has. You love him. And you have barely even explored the romantic side of Christian. If this works out, you are going to give him your all. Which means that there will not be any hiding your feelings. Which means that you will have to face your biggest fear; telling your parents the truth about you. That you love a man.*

Usually, the thought of telling his parents the truth about himself, the side of him that he had always kept hidden from them, would send every cell in his body to go into a shocking frenzy. Even now, Eli could feel a small twitch in his hand.

But then he thought of Christian. And the feeling either subsided, or Eli didn't care anymore. That was how powerful Eli's feelings for Christian were. Yes, he might not get the reaction from his parent that he would like, but at least he would be happy.

Happy.

Eli had never wanted to admit it, but hiding this secret from his family and friends had not made him happy. It made him feel as if he was only living half of his life out. The thought of being able to be who he was, all of who he was, stirred feelings in him that he had never felt before. Foreign, but not unwanted.

When Eli turned off the main road, and started riding on the road towards the walkway, Eli could instantly make out Christian's blue Nissan truck, with Christian leaning on the bed.

He is so handsome.

Eli parked and wasted no time getting out of the car. He wanted to hear what Christian had to say.

"Hi," Eli said as soon as he got out of the car.

"Hi," Christian repeated, but not as enthusiastically as Eli had been.

"I'm glad that you wanted to talk in person."

"Yeah, thanks for coming," Christian started. "Listen, I—"

"Please, Christian," Eli interrupted, "Please let me go first."

Before he could get Christian's approval, Eli began.

"I just want to say I'm sorry. I'm sorry for the awkward conversation earlier today. I'm also sorry for not being honest with you. I knew you weren't ready to date, but at the same time, I was developing these feelings for you. It's been a real struggle for me, but I think you are the one for me." Christian tried to interrupt again, but Eli continued. "I like you Christian. No, I don't like you. I *love* you. And my only regret now is that I didn't tell you sooner."

Eli smiled and sighed a breath of relief. It was nice to get it all out and in the open. He felt free.

Christian looked away, and didn't say anything for a long time. Finally, Eli tried to get a response out of him. "Christian, are you alright?"

Christian slowly turned to Eli. His personality that Eli was used to, the personality that Eli loved, wasn't there. Immediately, Eli realized that Christian hadn't asked him to meet him to confess his feelings for him.

It was much worse than that.

"Eli …Eli, I can't see you anymore. I can't talk to you anymore either."

It was as if Eli was standing in front of an oncoming train. There was nothing he could do, except stand there and wait for it to run over him.

And then it hit him.

"What?" Eli asked, almost gasping. He couldn't believe it. He hadn't seen this coming.

"I told you that I like someone else," Christian said. "And I may not just like him. Maybe I have the same feelings for him that you have for me. It's real. And I'm not going to ignore it."

Eli could feel the tears swelling up in his eyes.

So this is what it feels like to have your heart ripped from your chest and crushed right in front of you.

Christian continued, "When I realized that you had feelings for me, I had debated on whether to stop talking to you. But I didn't want to. You were a great friend to me. I enjoyed talking to you. But then today, I realized that your feelings for me are too much to ignore. Neither of us can pretend that they don't exist. And I can't try to be a friend to you when you want more than that."

Eli couldn't help it anymore. A large tear dropped down his cheek.

"Please don't cry," Christian said, "I'm not worth crying over."

Eli tried to catch all of the tears that were starting to escape. He started rubbing his face until his eyes started getting puffy and irritated. "Why shouldn't I cry? The guy that I like just told me that he not only doesn't want to pursue a relationship, he doesn't want to keep the friendship that we have. The friendship that I treasure. And it's not like you're all innocent. You gave me every signal that you liked me back. And then you leave me like this."

"I'm sorry."

"No you're not," Eli responded. He wiped his nose, now realizing that he was a total mess.

Christian didn't say anything, but Eli knew that what he had said had hurt Christian. He wanted to apologize as soon as he said it, but Christian was already moving and getting into his truck.

Eli stood there, speechless. He couldn't believe that this

was it.

All he could do was stand there as he watched Christian put the truck in reverse and drive away.

Chapter Twelve

It had been two weeks since that night when Eli's spirit was broken. Fortunately for him, the rest of the house was already asleep when he had returned home that devastating night.

Even though he was able to hide the initial breakdown from his family, he wasn't able to hide the change in his mood.

His mother finally could no longer take it. "Eli," she said, putting her drink down on the dining room table. "What is wrong? You've been like this for two weeks now."

He had decided to tell his parents about his sexuality the night that he had met Christian, but since that went to hell, Eli had no intention on telling his parents the truth. So of course, he couldn't tell them that he was sad because a man decided not to pursue a relationship with him.

"I'm just tired, mom," he responded, hoping that his excuse would work. "In case you haven't noticed, I have had lot of work to do in order to graduate. No sleep can affect a person."

After a few seconds, it looked as if his mother was buying his excuse. "Okay. But you should really get some rest. I don't want my baby so exhausted that he's dead before graduation."

"I'll try," Eli said as he left the table and went upstairs.

***

It had been two weeks, and there had been no word from Christian. Graduation was nearing closer every hour. But even though it was one of the most important moments in Eli's life, he was no longer able to enjoy it. Because the person he wanted to celebrate it with was no longer in his life. Although the urge certainly was there, Eli refrained from messaging the man. It was clear that he didn't want to talk to Eli. So why should Eli have to feel rejected, again?

All he wanted to do though was to get inside the man's head. He wanted to find out what he was thinking, and maybe get some insight into his situation with Eli. Then it hit him. If there was one place that Christian would go to share his feelings and not be judged about it, it was where Eli knew where to look.

He ran to his computer and started going through his browse history. He only hoped that he could still find the site. He turned on some music in the background and started searching on his computer.

He was relieved to find out that his computer still remembered the Equalitychat website. He clicked on it and immediately starting browsing for posts that Christian may have made since Eli had last searched the site.

He was shocked to find a thread that Christian had posted only a few hours after he had met Eli on the walkway. The night he broke Eli's heart.

It was obvious that Christian was upset at the time, because his thread title was *I Need to Vent*. Eli clicked on the thread and started reading what Christian had to say.

I'm sorry guys, I know you probably don't want to read every little detail of my life, but I am so worked up tonight, I need to vent my thoughts, and hopefully you can give me some insight.

Eli continued reading the long message that Christian had

written.

I never thought that my life would turn like this. I thought that I would be like everybody else: marry a girl, have kids, and ride off into the sunset in happiness. But after the terrible breakup with the girl of my dreams, everything changed. I started finding myself attracted to the same sex, something that once made me sick to my stomach.

Eli was shocked to read these things that Christian had written. It certainly wasn't something that he was used to see coming from Christian's bright personality.

I was confused with myself and my surroundings. I started looking at guys for the first time ever and asking, "Is he cute?" When it dawned on me that I did think these guys I was looking at were cute, I started thinking "That's sick. I should feel ashamed of myself. He is a guy."

Eli knew that Christian had been struggling with his sexuality for some time, but he had no idea how badly he had thought of himself because of these feelings that he had been having.

I started searching through the internet, trying to find an explanation for all of this. It had to be a phase, a moment of weakness because of my vulnerablility after the breakup. I couldn't be attracted to guys! I found this site and had some the best advice given that I have ever had. I felt at peace with myself, so at peace that I began to look for people like me that I could hang out with. I made a POF account, looking for friends and thought if something crazy awesome happens, then maybe more could happen. I talked to a lot of guys.

Eli instantly realized the part was reading was referring to him.

The first guy was pretty cool. We had several things in common and things were great. I saw him as a friend and nothing more. I made that clear to him, which I thought would make him feel otherwise. Before I knew it, I had met, Jaden. He asked me if I wanted to go out with him. Even though I knew the other guy wanted to go out with me, I went to eat with Jaden, and then went to the movies.

Eli could feel himself getting mad and upset at the same time. It hurt him to know that Christian had no problem passing over him for someone else, even though he knew that Eli liked him in some capacity. It appeared that Christian knew about Eli's feelings long before the time that he admitted.

I felt something click with Jaden. He was so perfect, so great that I had never felt anything like it before. I got butterflies and all those romantic feelings. Then the other guy asked me if I wanted to go hiking. I contacted him and said that I didn't feel right going on the trip.

Everything started to click with Eli.

Then today, he flat out asked me out, and confessed his real feelings for me. I said I wanted to remain friends, but the conversation quickly became awkward and I could tell he wanted more. He asked several times about my feeling towards the guy I was dating.

Dating? Eli's thoughts were starting to explode inside. Christian had only told him that he liked the guy. He didn't say anything about dating the guy. Apparently, Christian was hiding more than Eli had ever suspected.

Time moved on and the conversation continued to feel so awkward. I began to realize I could not be just friends with this individual who liked me in a different way and wanted more. I did what I thought I had to do and ceased talking to him.

So the truth lay right before Eli. Christian didn't have feelings for Eli, and he never did. Even after the time that had passed since Christian had broken Eli's heart, it still hurt to think or read anything by the man. Tears started to stream down his face. Eli quickly got up and locked the door to his room. There was no way that he wanted his family to catch him crying like he was.

Even though he knew that it would cause him more pain and heartache, he continued scrolling through the many posts that Christian had made on the forum. Eli then came across a post that was made only a few days ago.

I just have to take a moment and say how happy I am with my boyfriend. He is so damn amazing and I'm crazy attracted to him. I took him with me to visit my mom down in Georgia the other day. She kept commenting on how much more I smile and laugh and said that when I talk about him, my voice takes a much softer tone.

Oddly, this didn't make him feel any more upset. Instead, it made Eli feel numb.

He is happy. But he isn't with me. I could have made him happy.

All of a sudden, Eli noticed a song that was playing in the background. It was a new song that Sam Smith had released. Eli had only heard it once or twice, but never understood the lyrics until now.

And I hate to say I love you, when it's so hard for me.

The lyrics instantly caught Eli's attention. It was as if Eli's own thoughts were breaking out into song.

And I hate to say I want you, when you
make it so clear you don't want me.

Eli closed out of the internet browser that held the many words by Christian. There was no use in reading anymore. He read what he needed to know.

I'd never ask you cause deep down, I'm
certain I know what you'd say.

Eli got up and laid down on the bed, afraid what the next words would be in the song.

You'd say I'm sorry, believe me, I
love you, but not in that way.

The words made Eli instantly think of Christian, and the stream of tears started to roll down his face again.

And I hate to say I need you. I'm so
reliant. I'm so dependant. I'm such a fool.

Eli felt so broken. He felt as if every reason for living had been taken away from him.

When you're not there, I find myself singing the blues.

Yes, Eli was laying here, stewing in his misery. But Christian was enjoying life, being with the man of his dreams.

Can't bear, can't face the truth.

No, Eli was going to have to face the truth sooner than later. And the sooner he could realize that he would never be with Christian, the better.

You will never know that feeling. You
will never see through these eyes.

Eli had made up his mind. Even though he felt broken, he decided then and there that he needed to break away from what was making him feel incomplete. He needed to break away from Christian.

I'd never ask you, cause deep down
I'm certain I know what you'd say.

Eli picked up his phone and started browsing through his contacts. He found Christian's entry, and opened it. Before now, Eli would have been excited to look up Christian's name. But now, it tore him up to look at it. He knew what he had to do.

You'd say I'm sorry, believe me, I
love you, but not in that way.

"Goodbye," Eli said. Nobody was around him to hear it, but Eli knew what it meant. He was saying goodbye to Christian, which was hard for him. But, he was also saying goodbye to the feelings that he had developed for the man, which was even harder.

Eli tapped the DELETE button on his phone. In a split second, Christian's contact information was erased, forever lost in cyber space.

The action provided no comfort for Eli, but he knew it had to be done.

Now all I can do is move on.

His thoughts didn't help, as he laid there in misery until

he fell asleep.

> *You'd say I'm sorry, believe me, I*
> *love you. But not in that way.*

Part Two
Four Years Later

Chapter Thirteen

Eli was busily writing notes down on his notepad as Dr. Roslin presented his ideas.

"I would like for that press release to go out as soon as possible, if you can get that done," Dr. Roslin smiled at Eli. The man in his late forties had been talking about the many different opportunities that the Forrester County school system could get a better reputation. In the few months since his hiring, Dr. Roslin had made a great effort to explore the different options to take the school system in a newer, better direction.

His age didn't show, masked by physical activity which resulted in a muscular build. Eli had no problem admitting that the man was attractive, but didn't even entertain the thought of going down that road. The man was his boss, and twice his age.

"It'll be no problem," Eli responded, getting up from his seat in Dr. Roslin's office and offered his hand.

Dr. Roslin took it and shook it, firmly but friendly. "Good work, as usual."

Eli smiled before heading out of the office.

He was immediately greeted with a smile as he exited the office and shut the door.

"I was wondering when you were ever going to get out of there," Tori said from her desk, taking her attention away from the computer in front of her.

"You know how Roslin is," Eli responded, plopping himself in a chair in front of Tori. "He's always got ideas to make us the best school system in the state."

Eli managed to get Tori the position of Executive Assistant to the Superintendent a year after he was offered the position of Public Relations Director. Both Eli and Tori were glad to see her finally out of *Arcade Hut*. The added bonus was that they were still able to work together. Now, with more money.

"Good luck with that," Tori said, picking up some papers from her desk and getting up, signaling Eli to get up and walk with her down the hall. "With all of the scandals that go on, it'll be hard to give this place a perfect reputation. But on the bright side, all of these scandals, and Roslin's ideas, keep you employed here."

"Oh yeah," Eli responded taking the lead outside of her office, "I'm not complaining in the least."

The two walked slowly together down the hall as Tori made her way to the staircase that went downstairs, and as Eli made his way back to his office that was on the opposite side of the building. The two were chatting about a disagreement that Tori was having with her recent fiancé, Chris. When Eli realized that it was going to be a long conversation, he pulled the two of them into the break room so they could sit down and give the issue proper attention.

"Can you believe it?" Tori asked no one in particular as she sat down.

"I don't know why you're so upset because Chris' dog mated with yours," Eli said, nonchalantly.

"Eli, I told you," Tori said, "I breed Sally with specific dogs. And then I sell them. And now that he has let Cham mate with my baby, she is going to give birth to a bunch of mutts!"

Eli couldn't help but laugh. "Tori, I guess this will be one of the sacrifices that you'll have to make after you marry Chris."

Tori slapped Eli on the arm when Eli started to laugh harder. "Shut up. Last time I checked, you have no right to judge me about my relationship with Chris. You haven't been with anybody in like forever."

Her words killed any good mood that Eli was in. He thought they were just joking amongst each other. Now, things were personal.

It had been four years since the traumatic episode with him and Christian. *Christian.* Even after all this time, the name brought excitement and pain to Eli's heart.

In the time since Eli's decision to emotionally break away from the man he had fallen so deeply for, he worked on trying to get over Christian and finding the person of his dreams. He had gotten involved in some discreet relationships, both with men and women, but none had given him the level of euphoria like Christian had. Unfortunately, Christian had set the standard for Eli, and since then, nobody had ever been able to reach that standard.

Eli thought about Christian often. He wondered how a man who lived so close to him, could completely disappear off the face of the earth. He even indulged in his reoccurring temptation and would search for the man online. Whether it was Facebook, Twitter, Instagram, POF, or Google searches, Eli would check to see if the man had randomly reappeared, or if new rumors of his whereabouts had surfaced. Nothing. Eli had considered the thought of going door to door until he would find someone that knew something of the man. But he decided against it. He thought that was a little too stalkerish.

The incident with Christian caused him to pull back on his

plans to be publicly open about his sexuality. Four years after the day he decided that he would tell his family the truth, and they still didn't know. After Eli left his family's home and moved into his own, it became easier not to tell them. But the idea that they still believed him to being a different person still lingered over his head every day.

There were only two comforts that got him out of the pit of depression that Eli called "Hurricane Christian."

The first comfort was Tori, who was there for him when no one else was able to. He finally caved after deciding not to pursue Christian anymore and told her everything about him. The only thing he couldn't provide was a photo of him, which Eli hadn't realized he didn't have until Christian was gone from his life. Tori provided the comfort that he needed, telling him that Christian was a pig and a jerk and didn't deserve the great things that Eli could have given him.

Then there was Sam Smith's album. As soon as he heard that random song in his bedroom, Eli knew it was heaven's way of saying that he wasn't the only one feeling these things in the world, and that while it may hurt, he was still alive. Eli would play those songs over and over, belting out the lyrics as if he had written them himself. While Tori was also a fan of Smith, she eventually got tired of hearing the songs over and over. But because she knew that the album was able to get Eli through the day, she decided to let it slide. As time passed, Eli was able to go without listening to the heartbreaking album that spoke to his heart and soul for long periods of time. But as soon as a thought of Christian would pass his brain, he would have to break out the old playlist.

Eli brought his thoughts back to the present. Tori was still talking about how the past was the past, and how he shouldn't let it ruin his chance for a bright future. He tried to forget her saying that getting laid would solve all of his problems.

"I'm fine," Eli said, finally waving off Tori's concerns. "You have to admit that things are great with me right now."

Tori nodded her head. "I'll agree with ya there. I guess as long as you're not breaking out the Sam Smith CD again, we should be in good shape."

"Give me a break," Eli said, "His music got me through some tough times."

"Don't get me wrong," Tori countered, "I'm a fan of his. Can't wait for his next album. And I loved that one. But listening to any CD the amount of times that you and I have heard his, will drive anyone crazy."

Eli nodded in agreement.

Tori then resumed to talking about her conflict with Chris, and how the engagement would be over if any of those puppies that were born turned out to be runts. Eli was even less interested in the story this time than the first time he had heard it. She got so into it, Eli wasn't even sure that she was talking to him at that point, or if she cared if he was there. Sometimes, she just had to sit there and rant until she got everything off of her chest.

When it appeared that she was done with her venting, Eli looked at her and asked, "Feel better?"

"Yes," Tori said, clutching her bosom, trying to gather her breath. "Sorry that I went on and on."

"No worries. Who said that I was listening to you?"

"You're an ass," Tori said. She looked at the papers that she had laid on the table and looked at her watch. "I better take these downstairs and get back up here before Roslin gets another brilliant idea. If I wasn't here to ground him, there is no idea what shape we would be in."

She smiled at Eli and walked out of the break room, leaving him laughing at the possibilities.

***

The next day, Eli sat at his desk, emailing his usual press contacts with information on the upcoming events that the school system was holding that the press would be interested in printing in the papers and online.

He had begun drafting a new email when a voice from down the hall caught his attention.

"You're most welcome, Mrs. Ledford," said the familiar voice, "Anything for my favorite customer."

That voice.

Eli's insides started doing unusual twists and turns. The idea of the person that was down the hall from his office caused him to go into orbit.

Eli quickly got up from his seat and almost ran out of his office.

When he first exited his office and stared down the hall, all he could see was the carpet and white walls all of the way down the other end of the building. There was no one there.

Then, all of a sudden, someone stepped out of a doorway.

And there he was.

Christian.

Eli could barely believe it. After all of the years that he had spent unsuccessfully trying to search for the man who broke his heart, the man all of a sudden reappeared into Eli's life. And right down the hallway from where he worked.

All Eli could do was stand there, speechless and frozen in place, staring at the man in front of him. It appeared that the same was happening to Christian, who had just made eye contact with Eli.

Time had been good to Christian in the four years that Eli hadn't seen him. He looked almost the same. If it was even possible, Christian looked more attractive.

The two stood there and stared at each other until Christian gave a horizontal smile, and turned around and walked away, disappearing from sight as he went down the staircase.

Eli wanted nothing more than to go and run after him. But he still couldn't move. The shock of seeing Christian had left him in the same place when he first saw the man. By the time he was able to feel his body again, he was sure that Christian was long gone and far away from the building.

He was saddened and felt so angry at himself for not doing something sooner. *I should have done something!*

He did find a little comfort when he realized that the one person that Christian had come to see was still where she was. He walked down the hall and took a right where Christian had entered Eli's view.

"Mrs. Ledford?"

Dana Ledford, a middle-aged woman with short reddish brown hair, lifted her head from looking down at her computer and looked at Eli. "Hi Eli," she said, smiling. "What's up?"

Eli stepped a little bit closer into her office, but stood near the door. He smiled, trying to hide his recent shock to his core. "That man who was just speaking to you, who was he? He sounded very familiar."

"Oh, that was Christian Lance . He came by to bring me my laptop that he fixed for me so I wouldn't have to pick it up at the end of the day."

"How nice of him," Eli said, faking a smile. "He fixed your computer?"

"Yeah, he does a great job. I have to go see him every once in a while to get rid of the little boogers that my kids put on my hard drive."

"Very nice," Eli said, starting to feel sad.

He got the degree that he worked for. And I never got to see him get it.

"Do you know him?" Mrs. Ledford asked, bringing Eli back to the present.

"I did," Eli said, "Many years ago."

Eli waved to Mrs. Ledford goodbye and started walking towards the other end of the building. He didn't stop until he reached Tori's office.

When Tori saw Eli enter her office and saw the sadness in his face, it raised concern in her. "What's wrong?"

Eli stuck his head in Dr. Roslin's office quickly before returning it to face Tori. "Where is Dr. Roslin?"

"He left for a meeting," Tori said, getting up and walking towards Eli, "Why are you wondering—why are you so upset?"

"Oh my God, oh my God, oh my God," Eli said, clutching

the sides of his face. Tori stood there, next to him, until he was able to speak.

"I saw him," Eli finally said.

"Roslin?"

"No!" Eli was starting to get frustrated. "Christian!"

"Christian?" Tori asked, unsure what he was talking about. Then it hit her. "Your Christian?!"

"My Christian!"

"Oh my God!" Tori was now starting to freak out as much as Eli was. "Sit down and tell me everything!"

Eli sat down as Tori returned to her seat and told her the whole story, including how they stood there, staring at each other.

"The slime ball," Tori said. "You would think that he could have at least said hey."

"Well, I didn't say anything either," Eli responded.

"Yes, but you didn't break his heart and stopped talking to him for four years."

Eli didn't say anything. All he could do was sit there and feel the wave of hurt that he had finally pushed away start to overcome him.

Tori could tell that Eli's emotional floor was about to crumble below him. She got up and walked to Eli to hug him.

As soon as Eli was put in Tori's embrace, Eli let out an excruciating sigh. "Thank you, Tori," he croaked. "I don't know what I would do without you."

Tori slightly shushed him so he would stop speaking, risking the tears to fall out at any moment. Tori grabbed Eli in a tighter embrace and said, "You now have my permission to break out the

Sam Smith album again."

***

Eli was relieved to finally get home from work that day. He was hardly able to accomplish anything after seeing Christian enter his workplace.

I thought I was over him. So why do I feel this way?

Once Eli opened the door to his home, he was instantly greeted by Marik, his grey and brown tabby cat. When Eli had moved out of his parent's home, and into the old home of his grandparents, he was not able to take Zane with him. So he had to settle with making a new furry friend after his departure from home.

"Hey, baby," Eli said, bending over and picking up his feline companion as the cat walked in between Eli's legs. "How was your day?"

Marik meowed, which to Eli, was either a "Hello," or "Feed Me." He had an idea which one it was.

"Okay, I hear you loud and clear." Eli set the cat down and went to the counter where the cat food was placed.

Once Marik was satisfied with the food in front of him, he started eating. Eli took a step back and sat on the stool nearby, petting Marik's head as he ate.

"Hopefully you had a better day than I did. Listen, I know you're neutered, but still, don't get involved with anybody. Trust me, it's no good."

Marik didn't acknowledge that he knew that Eli was talking to him. Eli got up and left Marik to finish his dinner.

Later that night, Eli was lying in bed, with Marik lying at the foot of the bed in front of him. In the background, he had Sam

Smith's *In the Lonely Hour* playing. Usually at this time of night, Eli would be long gone into the depths of sleep. But tonight, he couldn't clear his mind long enough to doze off.

We haven't spoken in four years, and Christian couldn't give me the courtesy of a hello.

Eli knew that he had destroyed the friendship between the two of them, and even the possibility of a relationship down the road. But Eli had always thought that before that point, they had gotten really close, even though they disagreed on what closeness meant. That should have been enough to at least start some small talk before Christian ran out of the building.

Eli tried to push those thoughts out of his head before more unwanted thoughts entered.

I wonder if he is still with Jaden.

The name kept playing in his mind. Even though he had never met the man who attracted Christian, nor had he ever saw a picture of him, Eli had always had hateful feelings towards him over the course of four years. All of those hateful, devilish feelings that developed years ago started taking over again, creating images in Eli's head of what he would do to the man if he ever did see him.

Then Eli regained control.

Get a grip over yourself. Don't feel this way. This Jaden guy didn't steal Christian from you. Nor did Christian leave you to be with Jaden. He made the decision to see where things went with Jaden instead of you. Yes, the way Christian went about it hurt your feelings, but chances are that he has been happy over these years while you have kept yourself in misery and unable to commit to anyone else. It's time to let things lie.

Could he do it? Could he bury the past and finally move on from the only person that he ever truly loved?

That question was still running through Eli's mind when he passed out from exhaustion.

Chapter Fourteen

The next morning dragged on for Eli. He believed it was the combination of mental and physical exhaustion that he burdened himself with the day prior. Fortunately for him, his workload for the day was light.

"Feeling better?"

Eli looked outside his office door to find Tori leaning on the door frame.

"Do I look like I am?" He responded back.

"You look like you replayed all of yesterday in your head last night."

Eli rested his head in the palm of his hand. "You'd be right."

"It'll get easier with time," Tori said.

Eli looked at Tori and tried to smile. "I hope you're right."

The two didn't say anything. Tori walked away, with Eli knowing that he had her full support.

***

Eli was in the zone and in the midst of his work routine when his office phone rang from behind him. He turned around and reached for the phone.

"This is Eli. "

"Good morning, Eli, this is Caroline."

"Good morning, Caroline," Eli responded to the receptionist downstairs. "How are you?"

"I'm well, thanks." She waited a few seconds before she spoke again. "I have a Christian Lance down here with me who wishes to speak to you. Shall I send him up?"

Eli couldn't process what Caroline had said to him.

Why did he come back?

"Eli? Are you there?"

Hearing Caroline's voice snapped him back into sanity. "Yeah, I'm sorry, I'm here. Of course, please send him up."

As soon as he put the phone back on its cradle, he went into frenzy mode.

What will I say? What will I do?

To help calm his nerves, he started trying to organize his desk in a hurry. It wasn't as messy as a desk in the public relations field would be. But still, it was too messy for Eli to want Christian seeing it.

Eli was in the midst of putting some papers in a file when a knock came at the door.

He turned his head to see Christian standing outside Eli's office door.

Is Christian really standing outside my door? The man I have wanted to see more than anyone else during the past four years?

"Hi," Christian said.

Well at least he has already said more than yesterday.

"Hi," Eli replied. They stood there and stared at each other for several moments. When Eli realized that Christian was waiting for Eli to invite him in, Eli set the folder in his hands down on the desk and held his hand out for the seat in front of him. "Please, come in. Have a seat."

Christian smiled and walked over to the seat across from Eli. Eli could feel every cell in his body bursting in anticipation for what Christian had to say.

"I hope I'm not interrupting your work."

Not what Eli was thinking as the first thing they had to say to each other, but it was something. "No, you're fine. It's a slow day."

"Good," Christian responded. He waited a moment then said, "Eli, I wanted to apologize."

"Apologize for what?" *Breaking my heart so many years ago?*

"For not saying anything to you yesterday. I was so surprised to see you, I didn't know what to say or do."

Eli was glad it wasn't just him. "Yeah, me too."

Oddly, Eli was able to keep his cool. He didn't tear up from the pain that he was feeling inside, nor was he running to cling to Christian and trying to make up for lost time. He was there. *Just there.*

Eli knew, though, that Christian hadn't gone out of his way to just apologize for being a zombie yesterday. There was something else that prompted Christian to come to Eli's work to see him.

"So can I be perfectly blunt and ask a question?"

Christian sat there and braced himself for the question that he knew would come. "Sure, what is it?"

"What's the other reason for coming here?"

"Can't a guy just come and say hey to a friend?" Christian asked.

"Sure," Eli said, "But you and I haven't been on friendly terms for quite a while."

Christian's head bowed in defeat. "Yeah, about that. When I saw you yesterday, I was instantly reminded about what happened between us, and that we didn't end things on a good note."

Christian looked at Eli and when he saw that he still had Eli's attention, he continued. "All night last night, I couldn't stop thinking about how much of an ass I was towards you."

Eli couldn't help but instantly become mesmerized by Christian's stare. His eyes, his face, his body, was as gorgeous as ever. And here he was, apologizing to Eli for the way he acted. Eli didn't think this day would ever come.

"So," Christian said, "As a peace offering, I would like to take you out to lunch and catch up. That is, if you're not mad enough to turn me down."

Eli pondered on the offer for a split second. Nothing would make Eli happier than to say yes and go see what kind of life Christian had lived for four years. But at the same time, the man caused a great deal of pain for Eli, so why should he just up and start thinking nice things about Christian just because the man's conscience had finally caught up with him?

He made up his mind. "Sure, that sounds great." At least he would finally find out what the guy had been up to in the four years since he went off the radar.

"Wonderful," Christian said, smiling that smile that was imprinted in Eli's mind. "Want to meet at *Café Stratta*, say noon?"

"Looking forward to it," Eli responded, reciprocating Christian's smile.

"Great." Christian got up and walked towards the door. Before he left Eli's eyesight, he turned around and leaned against the door frame. "Eli?"

"Yeah?"

"I forgot to say that you look real good."

Eli didn't know how to take that comment, but for the moment, he decided to be polite and accept the compliment that was thrown at him. "You too."

***

"Holy crap!" Tori squealed, quickly covering her mouth so Dr. Roslin couldn't hear anymore in the next room. "You have to be kidding me!"

"I'm as serious as a heart attack," Eli replied. "He came up to my office, apologized for the way things went down between us, then asked if I wanted to go to lunch with him."

Tori still didn't understand. "What is his agenda by doing all of this out of the blue?"

"I have no idea," Eli shrugged. "But I guess I'll find out when I meet him later."

Tori ran past Eli, her black hair flinging all over the place, and blocked Eli's exit from her office. "Wait a minute," she said, her face as stern as a rock. "You mean to tell me that you're actually going to meet him?"

"Sure, I don't see the problem in that."

"The problem," Tori emphasized, putting her hands on her hips, "Is that this guy hurt you, on so many levels. And now you're just willingly letting him back into your life so he can hurt you again."

"I don't think—"

"No!" Tori said with a loud and firm tone. "What you should do is turn him down the same way he turned you down, and then give him the same painful feeling that he has inflicted on you for such a long time!"

Eli put his hands on her shoulders to give her a peaceful

state of mind. Her huffing and puffing started to ease up. It amazed Eli that it was he who was calm about this.

"Tori," he said, softly. "You know I love you. And I know you are just looking out for me. But all this time, I have been hurting because I didn't know what I was missing out on. I think that I have to see him this one last time to get the closure I need, and to move on."

Tori sighed in defeat. She knew that there was no way of convincing him not to go.

"Will you kick him in the groin if he starts playing his old tricks on you again?"

"I can promise you that," Eli smirked.

***

Eli pulled up at *Café Stratta* and put the car in park. But instead of getting out, he sat there and pondered if what he was doing was the right thing.

Are you prepared to get your heart broken again?

Eli thought about it long and hard before he thought, *My heart's already broken.*

That settled his personal conflictions.

He got out of the car and started heading towards the restaurant door. On his way, he looked around for the blue Nissan truck that Christian had had so long ago. But it was nowhere in sight. Either he wasn't here yet, or he had gotten a new vehicle.

As soon as Eli stepped inside, he saw him.

Christian was located at the very back of the restaurant, but in clear view from the front. For a moment, Eli thought that he chose that spot because he wanted to be discreet. But that flew out of his idea as quickly as it had come in. Christian had been out for years.

"Thanks for coming," Christian said as Eli sat in the booth across from him.

"I wouldn't miss it," Eli replied.

"I'm glad you say that." Christian smiled, and then said, "I wouldn't have blamed you if you didn't want to come."

"Well, I have to admit that you're not the only one with an agenda today."

"Really?" Christian had a curious look on his face. "What is *your* agenda?"

"I want to know what has happened to you over the last four years."

At that point, their waiter walked up to them. Eli actually knew the guy. His name was Aaron. They had went to school together many years ago. But while Eli graduated and got a college education, Aaron got a girl pregnant before they were eighteen, so he dropped out to provide for his new family by working as many minimum wage jobs as possible.

"Hi, Eli," Aaron said. Eli had talked to him while they were in school together, but he had no idea they were that close. "What can I get you to drink?"

"I'll have a Sprite," Eli said, then looked at Christian. "What about for you?"

Christian looked at Eli, smiled, and then looked at Aaron. "I'll have water, please."

Aaron walked away with their drink order and went in the kitchen towards the back. When he disappeared, the two at the table resumed their conversation.

Eli decided to resume. "So I hear that you work on computers. I guess you got your degree. Congrats."

"Thanks," Christian responded. "I graduated the spring of 2015, so I've been working at *Computer Central* ever since. What about you, though? You graduated in 2014 with a PR degree. Congrats to you!"

"Thanks," Eli said, chuckling. "I didn't think you'd remember."

"Of course I remember. Plus, I see your name in the paper all the time as a representative for the school. You keep yourself busy."

The conversation with Christian was going super well, Eli thought. It was as if nothing had changed. As if a time warp took them before that horrible night in 2014, and brought them here, four years later. As if nothing had happened.

"Yeah, I guess so."

The two sat there for awhile. Aaron brought them their drinks and took their lunch order. Eli was looking at his work email on his phone when Christian spoke up.

"Go ahead and ask."

Eli had no idea what he was talking about. "Ask what?"

"Ask me the question you're dying to ask. About my love life over the last few years."

How is it that he can read my thoughts like an open book? "What makes you think that I want to ask about that?" Eli questioned.

"Because I want to know the same thing about you," Christian responded, keeping his eyes on the table. Hearing that comment put Eli's insides in a whirlwind. "Besides, it was our love lives that put us where we are now; almost strangers after all this time."

Eli wanted to point out that it was Christian who put the two of them down this path, even though he knew that while Christian did start the catalyst, Eli did drive them to that point.

"Okay, fine," Eli caved in. "What's happened since we stopped talking?"

Christian took a deep breath, as if he was bracing from something bad. "Well, I decided to get together with Jared."

Tell me something I don't know.

"It was a perfect fit. Like a match made from heaven. I instantly fell for him, I guess the same way that you fell for me."

That comment left Eli speechless. When he didn't say anything, Christian continued speaking.

"And after I graduated, we got married."

Hearing that did prompt a response from Eli. "You WHAT?!" Eli briefly looked down at Christian's left hand and didn't notice a wedding band on his finger.

Christian smiled. "What's the shocking reaction for? You know that men have been allowed to marry each other in North Carolina since late 2014."

"I know," Eli responded, "But out of all of the times that I've thought about you over these years, I never thought that you would get married."

"Believe me, it was a shock for me too," said Christian. "He swept me off my feet without me even realizing it."

Even though it made Eli angry that he wasn't able to say the same, seeing Christian happy made him happy. "It sounds perfect."

Christian nodded his head. "It was. He was the love of my life."

Eli was confused after hearing him say that. Surely he heard it wrong. Then he couldn't help but notice once again that a wedding band was not on the man's finger. "You say that in past tense."

"Yeah."

Eli watched Christian as his mood and personality changed right in front of Eli. He was no longer the happy person that Eli remembered, nor was he the man who worshiped his husband. Something wasn't right. And the tensing of Christian's body was proof that something was off.

"Christian?" Eli asked with some concern in his voice, "Is something wrong?"

The man in front of him took a few deep breaths before finally saying, "Jaden passed away about a year and a half ago."

Eli was not expecting that response. He felt horrible, and he didn't even know the man he felt sorry for. He could only imagine how Christian was feeling.

"Oh my God, Christian, I am so very sorry."

Christian looked up at Eli. He hadn't shed a tear, but it was obvious that he had shed many tears about his deceased husband over the passing time. "Thank you, Eli. That means a lot to me."

Eli smiled with sympathy, but didn't say anything. There was something that was nagging at him.

"I don't want to pry," Eli started, "But how did he pass?"

"Hodgkin's Lymphoma," Christian said.

"Oh my gosh," Eli said, his head shaking with sympathy. "I'm sorry to hear that."

Christian decided that instead of responding to Eli, he

would continue with the story that had much more to it. "He was diagnosed a little more than a year after our wedding. He had just graduated from college in Asheville. He was so excited about getting his first job. He went for a degree in nursing."

Eli was at a loss for words. Christian's story was heartbreaking.

Christian's head started to sink even lower than earlier. It was as if the pain he was feeling was causing him to ball up in the fetal position. "He never got to work one day though. While the doctors said that it was treatable, and that he was going to make it, he just kept getting worse. Every day, I sat there and watched him waste away. Towards the end, he was ready to die. And I sat with him until he passed."

Eli was surprised that they both weren't in tears. That was certainly the saddest story that he had ever heard. It sounded like Christian had had a rough couple of years as well. Who would have known that the both of them would have been hurting?

Eli tried to say something to comfort Christian, but nothing could come out. "I...I don't know what to say."

Christian shrugged. "You don't have to say anything," Christian said. "I can tell from the look on your face that you're sorry. And I thank you for your concern. But I'm okay. We loved each other, and we were there for each other until the end. He also said—"

Christian was interrupted by Aaron, who had finally arrived with their food. Whether it was five minutes that had passed, or fifty, Eli wasn't sure.

"Thank you," Eli and Christian said together, and smiled when they realized that they said it at the same time.

Aaron walked away and Eli took a bite from his sandwich. "What were you saying?"

It was as if Christian was ready to say something, but then changed his mind. "Oh, it was nothing."

Eli nodded his head and took another bite. Christian did the same.

When Christian was done taking his first bite, he set his sandwich down.

"So what about you?"

"Huh?" Was all that Eli could reply. He had no idea what Christian was talking about.

"How has your love life been over the years?"

Eli didn't want to be truthful. But he thought that if Christian was completely honest with him, then he should be the same way. "Well, to put it simply, it's been pretty nonexistent."

Christian couldn't believe it. "You're kidding?"

Eli shook his head. Then he said, "You know, I've met some people," Eli stuck his finger out to keep Christian from interrupting him, "Both guys and girls. And I don't know, I just haven't met the right person."

Christian folded his arms, acting all confidently. "Don't worry, Eli, I know there is someone out there for you. And you're going to make him or her the luckiest person in the world."

Eli was surprised by that statement. Did Christian know something that Eli didn't?

The two of them sat there and finished their lunch. In between, they talked small talk and discussed what their jobs entailed.

Eli hated it, but a rush of old feelings started to creep up on him again. It was as if nothing had happened between the two of them. But he knew that things had happened. Christian had gotten married, and watched the love of his life die from a terrible disease. Christian was in no way ready to meet someone else, especially someone who had loved him years ago, even though he didn't share the same feelings.

Eli knew that this was the exact thing that Tori had warned him about.

Aaron came and started picking up the cleaned plates on the table. "Is there anything else I can get for you?" He asked, pulling the check out of his apron.

Eli shook his head. Christian looked at Aaron and reached for the check, saying, "I'll take that."

Eli tried and reached for it, but Christian pulled it too far for Eli to reach. "Please, Christian, it's my treat."

"No sir," Christian responded, smiling. "The deal was that I would take you to lunch if you forgave me for what happened between us. Do you forgive me?"

"Well, yes," Eli said, honestly.

"Well then this is my treat. You can get the next one." Christian winked at Eli.

Eli couldn't help but get the same feelings he had when he first saw Christian after high school. He couldn't get a read off of the man, and couldn't tell if he was being particularly flirty with him, or if he was a flirt in general.

"Well, thank you. I really enjoyed it."

Once Christian paid at the front register, the two men

walked out together. Eli was still unsure where Christian parked.

"Where are you parked?" Eli asked.

Christian pointed towards the nearby red and black Kia Soul that was parked at the front of the restaurant.

"Nice car," Eli said.

"Thanks," Christian said. "Not only is it a nice looking car, but it is also electric."

"You're kidding. I've always wanted one of those."

Christian shrugged his shoulders jokingly. "It just made good since to me. But because it only drives so far on just electric, I kept the little blue Nissan for those long trips."

Another cold case solved, Eli thought.

Eli started stepping towards the direction of his car, which was in the opposite direction. He had completed his deal with Christian, so he was unsure what to do next. It wasn't as if things all of a sudden changed back to the way things were before, as much as Eli wanted it to. "Well thanks so much for lunch. I had a great time catching up." He looked down at his cell phone and put it back in his pocket. "But I gotta go. I took more time for lunch than I should have."

"I understand completely," Christian said, nodding his head in agreement. But instead of waving goodbye, which is what Eli would have done, he held out his hand to shake Eli's. So many emotions and memories washed over Eli, remembering the night that he met Christian for the first time at the Asian restuarant. The night he knew that Christian was the one for him.

Or the one he had thought was for him.

But just because he was overwhelmed by the past, didn't

mean that it should affect his present. Yes, Christian apologized for what happened, and he took Eli to lunch as a peace offering. But the fact remained: Christian didn't feel the same way about Eli as Eli felt about him.

The least I can do is shake his hand goodbye and walk away with dignity. Maybe I'll get the closure that I've been searching for all these years.

Eli walked up to Christian and put his hand in Christian's. "It was good to see you again. Take care."

Christian shook Eli's hand and said, "Yes, you too."

But instead of letting go and parting ways, Christian grabbed Eli's hand tighter and then pulled him closer to Christian. The two stood there, hand in hand, close enough to be kissing.

What does this guy think he is doing?

"Eli," Christian said, before taking a breath and saying, "Can I see you again?"

Eli couldn't believe it. It was as if his heart went from a normal pace to racing like a jack rabbit in heat.

"You want to see me again?"

"Yes," Christian responded, looking Eli directly in the eyes. "I want to make up for lost time."

Eli wasn't exactly sure what the man meant by that. Possibly he just wanted to reunite their friendship. He was four years late on that, but better late than never.

"That sounds great," Eli said.

Christian broke away from his handshake from Eli, breaking the lingering spell that the close encounter had on Eli. He got Eli's number and started walking away, towards his car, but not taking his eye off of Eli. "It's a deal then. I'll text you real soon!"

Eli waved goodbye, then started walking over to his car, unsure what today's event meant, for either of them.

＊＊＊

Eli was in the kitchen, preparing several dishes when Tori's voice came from in the hall.

"Can I help you with anything?"

"No, I'm good," Eli said. He picked up the bowls of chips and Chex Mix and started walking down the hall to the living room, where Tori was.

As soon as Eli returned from his lunch with Christian, Tori was there to interrogate him. Instead of dishing out the details where someone could overhear, he invited her to his house to give all of the details. Tori insisted that he tell her then, but all Eli would say was "It was great."

Before Eli event stepped into the living room, Tori was asking questions.

"Tell me what happened."

"Hello to you too," Eli said sarcastically. He set the bowls down on the table in front of them and started telling the story.

Tori didn't say anything until Eli was completely finished with a detailed list of the day's event. He even included the parts where Christian got close and personal, giving Eli feelings that he hadn't felt in a long time.

"So, what do you think?"

Tori sat there and pondered on what she wanted to say before she gave her response. "I really don't know, Eli. I mean, yes, his story about his sick husband is convincing and sad, but his actions towards you may just be his old self playing you."

Eli had come to the same conclusion that Tori had made. It was a very good possibility that the man hadn't changed over the years, despite his circumstances.

He got up and started pacing the room, frustrated that neither of them could make sense of the events that occurred that day. "What if we are looking at it wrong? I talked to him like a long-lost friend. I don't think that we were acting like love interests."

Tori shrugged, taking in Eli's thoughts as a possibility. "But what about 'Can I see you again?' Not a lot of guys who are just friends pull you closer and ask you that, whether you are gay, bi or straight."

Eli grunted in frustration. What he thought would have been a day of closure, turned out to be a new line of questions and unsolved answers.

Seconds afterwards, Eli's phone vibrated on the table.

"Who is it?" Tori asked as Eli sat back on the couch to pick up the phone.

His insides turned over when he read who the text message was from.

"It's Christian," was all that he could say.

Tori sat up straight, eager to find out what Christian had on his mind. "What does it say?"

"He asked, 'Want to hang out tomorrow after work? Maybe take a walk on the walkway?'"

Tori's eyes got big. "What are you going to say back?"

He sat there and weighed his options. No matter what happened, he needed to find out what Christian's interest in being around Eli was. Whether it resulted in the two of them becoming friends, more than friends, or nothing, he had to find out the truth.

Eli started responding to Christian and pressed SEND when he was done.

Tori was clueless what was going on, and she looked like she was dying inside from the suspense. "What did you say?"

Eli didn't respond. All he did was hold his phone up so Tori could read the message he sent.

I'm down.

Chapter Fifteen

As soon as five o' clock rolled around the next day, Eli had everything packed up and was ready to leave the office.

Eli was unable to do anything but think about Christian and the confusing interaction that they had had together the day before. Tori's advice wasn't helpful, nor was the different scenarios that played in Eli's head.

He rushed to get to his car without stopping and talking to anybody as he was leaving. He was on a mission, and he wasn't going to be late.

As Eli was driving towards the walkway, he tried predicting the different directions that this new meeting could go. It was the same place where Christian broke his heart so long ago. So right off the bat, it was a bleak outlook. But Eli couldn't help but think about how different Christian had acted towards him yesterday. Sure, he was his same flirtatious self, but the man's apology seemed sincere. Maybe he was trying to make amends from his past actions, and the walkway was an ironic, symbolic place to do that.

Eli's thoughts were still all over the place when he pulled into the walkway. Not much had changed to the place in the four years since he had been there. He never returned after that traumatic night, feeling that going back there would bring back old feelings. And he was right. He could start to feel the hurt, the disappointment, and the tears that he shed right there in the parking area.

Christian was already there, as usual. Some things never changed. He brought his old, blue Nissan truck instead of the Soul.

And like Eli had always seen him, he was leaning against the truck.

Eli got out of the car. Christian was by his side before Eli realized that the man had moved so quickly.

"Hi," Christian said with a smile from ear to ear. "It's good to see you again."

"It's good to see you too," Eli said, "Although the location isn't the best place."

Christian nodded and said, "I figured you would have hard feelings towards this place. To be honest, I haven't been here since the terrible thing I did to you right here. But don't worry, I have no intention of doing that to you today."

"In that case," Eli said, clearing the way for Christian to walk in front of him, "Lead the way."

The two men started walking towards the paved trail, Eli eventually catching up to Christian and walking alongside him.

They were silent for a long time. Eli was rather uncomfortable by the silence. His only comfort was watching the creek flow in the opposite direction from where they were walking. Eventually, the silence was too much. He had to know why he was here.

He stopped right in his tracks. If there had been anyone behind him, they would have tripped right on top of him, and Lord knows what else. Christian hadn't noticed, and was still walking when Eli called out his name. Christian turned around, a confused look on his face for why they had stopped.

"Christian," Eli started, "Why am I here? Why are you here? Why have you suddenly changed your tune about me after you made it very clear where we stood years ago?"

Christian stood there with his hands on his hips. "I told

you that I want to make amends for what I did to you."

Eli shook his head, rejecting the excuse. "No, you made amends yesterday when you apologized and took me out to lunch. Most people who made things right between two people usually go about their business. But you, you are pushing yourself back into my life. And I need to know why."

Christian looked at the trail that he wished he was walking. "I was hoping we could walk awhile before we got to that part."

So he's promising me to tell me the truth?

"So you'll tell me what's going on if I follow you on this trail?"

"Exactly. Everything."

Eli agreed and started walking again. He had come too far to leave without an explanation.

They walked for what seemed like forever. But Eli never said anything. The silence was killing him, but he knew that his prize waited for him at some point on this trail. He didn't bother to offer small talk or anything like that. He hoped by not saying anything, he could force Christian to talk in order to escape his own awkward silence.

After several more minutes, Christian pulled Eli to the side and sat them both down by the nearby bench.

"Okay, I'm ready."

"Okay," Eli said, please that he was finally going to get his answers. "I'm all ears."

Christian took a deep breath before saying, "Eli, you remember what happened here, four years ago, right?"

Eli looked at him like he was an idiot. "Uh, yeah."

Christian chuckled at Eli's response. "Yeah, that was obviously a dumb question. What I'm trying to say is that telling you that I couldn't speak to you then was just as painful for me as it was for you."

Eli still didn't understand the man. "Please explain, because I'm so lost."

Christian sighed again. "What I'm trying to say is that I had feelings for you back then."

Eli couldn't move or say anything. It was as if someone had come up to him and given him news that he dreaded hearing. Except he wanted to hear this. It was something that he had wanted to hear for years. But he couldn't seem to grasp that Christian had just said the words.

"Eli?"

Eli came out of his trance. But things still didn't add up for him.

"As flattered as I am to hear that," Eli said, "I don't believe it. You had feelings for Jaden. That's why you didn't want to speak to me or be in my life."

"You're only half right."

Eli stared at Christian. He didn't know what to say or ask.

"Okay," Christian caved in, deciding to tell the whole story. "I lied to you about everything. I lied about freaking out when I realized that you had feelings for me. I lied about just wanting to be friends with you. In fact, I was so happy when I knew about your feelings, because I was feeling the same thing. And I didn't want to just be friends with you. I wanted a relationship with you."

Eli's eyes were glazed over. He was so overwhelmed; he could barely process the information that was being thrown at him.

"The only problem is that I didn't realize it until after Jaden died."

Things were finally making sense to Eli now.

"You see, I also lied about when I met Jaden. I met him long before you confessed your feelings toward me. So by then, I was madly in love with the man, and unable to feel the same things that you felt towards me. Also, I was very emotional during the whole loving a man and trying to come out process. Which is probably why I didn't respond to you the way I should have."

Eli could understand that. He knew that it was an emotional rollercoaster, and he hadn't even come out yet.

Christian continued to talk, unaware of what Eli was thinking inside. "After Jaden died, I felt so broken and alone. I didn't think I could ever have a relationship with someone again. Both my friends and my mom tried to set me up with people, but I never went through with it. The only thing that was able to make me feel whole again was to think of you."

Did he really just say that?

"By that time, I had no way of getting in touch with you. I didn't even know if you were still in the area. I figured that you would have gotten over me and moved on with a person that de-served you. "

Eli's head sank, feeling sad for himself for never moving on and finding someone that could have made him happy.

"But then I saw you at your office."

That perked up Eli's attention, causing him to lift up his head and resumed listening to Christian.

"When I saw you only two days ago, all of those feelings

rushed back. I never expected to see you again. But when I did, I didn't know what to do or say."

Hearing those words coming from Christian made Eli feel so special.

"Eli," Christian said with a serious tone in his voice, "I'm very sorry about what happened between us. It was certainly not my intention to hurt you. I guess you do things you normally wouldn't do when you're in love. I chose to be with Jaden. I don't regret that decision, and I never will. But I do regret cutting you out of my life and putting us in the position that we're in now."

Eli could still feel every ounce in his body being overwhelmed. But now, he was starting to feel something that he had been waiting for years: closure. It was as if the lingering hole in his soul was starting to heal, something that he never thought could happen.

"I...uh..." Eli was near speechless, but he knew that he had to say something. "I don't know what to say."

Christian chuckled from Eli's response. "You don't have to say anything." He once again took the lead on the conversation. "I know this is all overwhelming to you. But I needed you to know everything that has happened over the years."

Once Eli was able to get his thoughts back in order, there was only one thing running through his head.

What next?

Eli decided against beating around the bush, and be up front and honest, just like Christian was being towards him.

"So," Eli started, "Why are you telling me all of this?"

"Because," Christian said, putting his hand over Eli's, indicating a romantic gesture. "I still have feelings for you, and I want to ask you out on a date."

Feeling Christian's hand over his sent Eli's mind into orbit. He could see and hear fireworks in his head, something that had never happened to him before.

"Wow" was all that Eli could say.

Christian nodded his head. "I know. That's all I've been able to say for the last couple of days."

Eli was still speechless, unable to comprehend that the man that he fell in love with years ago, shared the same feelings towards him. He always had.

Eli was unaware that Christian was talking to him until Christian said "So?"

Hearing Christian's words brought him back to reality. "So what?" He asked.

Christian shook his head, smiling. Eli knew that his look was a look of need; needing and wanting Eli. Eli still couldn't understand what it was about himself that made Christian act the way that he had been acting for the last couple of days.

"You know," Christian said, "You should really stop being so speechless. I know I just dropped a bombshell on you, but come on; I'm not worth losing the power of speech."

I seriously doubt that.

"So let me ask again, since you didn't hear me the first time: Will you do me the honor of going on a date with me?"

I'm dreaming. I have to be dreaming.

But in fact, he wasn't. And instead of learning the hard way by pinching himself, he decided to let it go and enjoy in his dreams that were finally coming true.

Eli started shaking his head no. And when Christian's head started to sink in disappointment, and Eli realized that he had the man in his joke, he said "Sure," smiling from ear to ear.

When Christian realized that he had been played, he punched Eli lightly on the shoulder. "You're such a tease."

Eli countered back with "I learned from the best," which caused both of them to smile. "Of course, I'll go on a date with you."

"Okay, good," Christian said, wiping his forehead with the back of his hand, acting dramatic. "You had me worried there for a bit."

By the time they finished their laughing and teasing, the sun was starting to set. The two got up from the bench that they were comfortable in, and started to walk back to the parking lot.

"Can I be honest with you about something?" Christian asked after they hadn't spoken for awhile. It was clear to Eli that Christian had been thinking for awhile. That was okay for Eli to walk in silence for a little bit. He had been enjoying just walking next to the man.

"Of course."

"I was almost stupid enough to not go to your office yesterday. A part of me thought that it was best if I didn't go back."

"Why was that?" Eli questioned.

"I don't know," Christian said. After a few more seconds of thought, he said, "I guess when I saw you, and I was overwhelmed by how hot you looked, I couldn't help but think that you had moved on and was happy with someone else."

Hearing Christian say the word "hot", especially when he referred to Eli, made things stir in Eli that he had never felt before. It wasn't lust. No, this feeling was more powerful than any feeling a hook-up could give him. This was *passion*. The thought of feeling those feelings so early after restoring connection with Christian scared him. He didn't want to scare him off, but at the same time, he wanted to cling to the man and never let go.

"It's a good thing you're not stupid then," Eli responded, nudging his shoulder with Christian's. He figured it was okay to be flirty with him. Christian had certainly been flirty with Eli since they met the day before. "Otherwise, we would still be in the same sad state that we were in before you regained your wits."

"Thank goodness I had my wits about me," Christian said, pointing his index finger at his head.

They finally reached the parking lot, and walked towards their cars. Eli was starting to get a surge of energy that was starting to spread all over his body. He wanted to do something exciting, something wild, and something that he had never done before. And he wanted to do it with Christian.

Eli took some deep breaths to calm himself down, though. There was no way he was about to ruin his connection with Christian again. And thinking things that neither of them was ready for yet was out of the question.

Eli leaned against his car, which prompted Christian to do the same. While Eli was looking in another direction, Christian reached out and grabbed his hand, which caught him off guard.

"I've got you safe in my hands," Christian said.

Eli wasn't sure what Christian meant by that, nor did he

care. But hearing him say those words made Eli look at him as a protector; as a hero even. The thought of having him in Eli's life forever made him believe that he could accomplish anything in the world with Christian at his side.

"You promise?" Eli asked.

"I promise."

Eli stood there, with his hand in Christian's and bathed in the warm feelings that were flooding his heart. He hadn't felt this warm inside since he realized his feelings for Christian years ago. He was glad to finally have those feelings back.

Chapter Sixteen

That Friday afternoon, Eli found himself spending a rather long time in the bathroom getting ready. He spent so long in there, Marik came in and jumped onto the counter to see what the fuss was.

"Daddy has a date," Eli said, kissing his beloved cat on the nose. After thinking about it for a moment, he realized that he probably needed to stop showing so much affection for the cat, for someone may misconstrue it as a substitution for a love interest. And calling himself "Daddy" had lost its charm too.

Thinking of his date this evening was the only thing he was able to think about since he and Christian parted ways at the walkway. He missed the feeling of Christian's hand. Holding it was such a simple gesture of affection, but to Eli, it meant a lot.

The two called and texted each other every chance that they got. A moment without reading a message from Christian was almost unbearable to Eli. It was as if his feelings for the man had come back as powerful as ever, if not more intense. Except this time, he could tell that Christian was feeling the same thing. Not questioning Christian's feelings was certainly a nice change.

He promised Christian that he would meet him in town at 6:30 that evening, and he would text him a specific location shortly before that. Which meant that he had to get a move on things, because it was already 5:30, and he wasn't completely ready.

Finally, after much frustration, and trying on almost every single button down shirt in his closet, he decided to go with his blue and black plaid shirt. He rushed back into the bathroom to put it on.

Before he put it on, he stood there and stared at his shirtless self in the mirror. Not much had changed since his extraordinary transformation after graduating high school. He was still muscular, and worked occasionally to maintain his figure. He could only imagine how Christian looked without his shirt on, and if Christian was thinking the same thing about him at his house.

Eli finally stopped staring at himself and began getting ready. He finally finished, putting every spike of gelled hair in its proper place, and went to go grab his keys from the kitchen counter. As he went to grab them, the door bell rang.

He grunted in frustration. Tori had probably come to bother Eli and either get the details on his date, or talk him out of going out with Christian. She had gone back and forth on her opinion of Christian ever since she found out that he was finally sharing the feelings that Eli had for him.

"Tori, please," he yelled as he walked towards the door, "I don't have time for you right now. I have to leave soon."

He opened the door and was shocked to not find Tori standing in front of him, but Christian.

Eli did a double take. "Christian, what are you doing here? I thought we were planning to meet in town in a half hour."

"That was the plan," Christian started, "But I've never been a fan of following the rules I set for myself. So I decided to pick you up."

Eli thought it was a sweet gesture, but he didn't understand something. "How did you find out where I lived?"

"Well," he said, smirking from embarrassment, "As soon as you left work today, I went in and said that I wouldn't leave until I saw your friend, Tori. When she finally came down to talk to me, I told her who I was, and said that I needed your address."

Uh oh. Eli knew that he would get an ear full from Tori sooner rather than later. "What did she say?"

"Well, she was kinda like you for a while. She was speechless for a long time. I had to ask the question several times before she realized I was there and could answer me."

It appeared that Tori had fallen for Christian's charms and good looks, just like Eli had.

"Anyways," Christian continued, "She told me where you live, and now, here I am."

Eli smiled. "I'm glad you're here. But you didn't have to come all the way out here. I could have met you in town."

Christian folded his arms and shook his head with disagreement. "Now, what fun would that be, when I could pick you up and surprise you instead?"

Eli smiled, stepped outside and shut the door behind him. "You're too much."

"I know, right?

Before Eli could open the door to Christian's *Soul*, Christian had his hands on the handle and pulled the door open for him.

"Wow," Eli said, sliding into the car. "I've never heard of a guy opening the door for another guy."

"I guess I'm not an ordinary person," Christian said as he shut the door and walked around the car to the driver's side.

When he turned the car on and they started going into

reverse, Eli's excitement was too much to contain.

"What is it?" Christian asked as he put the car into drive and drove out of Eli's driveway.

"Well, I have my Civic Hybrid, so I know what it's like to drive on a battery at times, but I've never driven in a car that was all electric."

Christian looked at Eli and winked. "I guess I'm introducing you to all sorts of things for the very first time."

"Yes, you are." And he hoped that there were a few other things that Christian would introduce him to for the first time. The thought sent tingles down below his waist.

Christian looked at the road that was now behind them. "You have a nice house. Do you own it or just rent?"

"I own it. But I still think of it as my grandparent's house."

Christian's look went from happy to concern. "What happened to them?"

"They both died about two years ago."

"Oh, Eli, I'm sorry," Christian said. "I shouldn't have asked."

Eli reached for Christian's hand, which was on the gear shift. "It's okay. You don't have to be sorry for asking me anything. It was their time, and I've accepted it, even though it can be hard at times."

"I know how that goes," Christian said.

Eli took his hand off of Christian's. He knew that Christian was referring to Jaden, and he didn't want to act romantic while the tone was so grim.

Would Christian think that he was betraying Jaden by going on a date with Eli? It was something that Eli hadn't thought about until that moment.

The awkward silence was killing him so much, he had to change the topic. "Actually, when you think about it, their passing was kinda romantic."

"How so?"

Eli readjusted his position in his seat in order to view Christian better while he told the story. "My grandmother died during the winter of 2016. She was exposed to the seasonal flu and never recovered from it. But no matter how sick she got, my grandfather would stay by her side and made sure he was there to help her with whatever she needed, even if it potentially exposed him to the flu as well.

"After she died, my grandfather's health started to drastically decline. He lost all energy and motivation to do anything. We would practically have to force him to eat something.

"It was less than a month after she died that he followed. The doctor said that he probably died from the same strain of flu that my grandmother died from. But I don't believe it."

Christian's confusion was apparent on his face, and he took his eyes off of the road long enough to look at Eli and ask, "What do you believe?"

Eli gave a long sigh, unsure if he should tell Christian and risk embarrassing himself. "I believe that he lost the will to live after she died. They were married for over sixty years. And I believed that his reasons for living died with her."

"That is certainly a possibility," Christian responded, "It is not uncommon to hear something like that."

Eli leaned back in his seat, deciding to get in a more comfortable position after telling Christian his story and theories. "I believe it's the truest form of love."

"It definitely sounds powerful," Christian said.

"I think that if anybody finds someone that they can spend the rest of their life with, and love them so much that it kills them to live a life without them, then that is true love."

"Think we will get that?" Christian asked, winking at Eli.

Eli rolled his eyes. Christian's flirting drove Eli wild, but in a good way. "Don't get me wrong, I like you, but this is just our first date."

"I'm very optimistic."

They drove through downtown Pinecrest and Christian finally pulled over where *Angel's* restaurant was. The dining was very elegant. Eli came here all the time with his parents when he still lived with them. But after he moved out, he never found the time to go with someone.

"Do you like Italian?"

"I love this place," Eli said. He couldn't help but smile. "You didn't have to bring me to such a ritzy place."

"What can I say," Christian said, raising his hands in defense, "I like to go all out on the first date."

They went inside. Eli held the door open for Christian, who patted a thanks on Eli's lower back. Eli looked inside and noticed that not much had changed in the years since he had been here.

"Hi," a busty woman said as she came out of the kitchen to welcome her new guests. She looked at Christian. "How many do we have tonight, hun?"

Christian held up two fingers and then he said, "Can we have a spot in the back?"

The hostess took them to the last table in the building, and laid their menus before them. "Sheila will be with you in a moment."

Christian and Eli nodded their heads and started looking at the menu. Eli knew already what he wanted, but continued to look through what they had to offer. "Do you come here often?"

Christian shook his head. "Jaden and I came here a couple of times. But after his diagnosis, we didn't get out much." Once Christian realized that he set the conversation on a sad note, he added, "But we loved it every time we came."

Eli nodded his head in agreement. "My family and I enjoyed it every time we came here as well."

Once Sheila came to their table, Eli ordered the regular spaghetti and meatballs, while Christian ordered the shrimp linguini. The waitress wrote everything down before turning around and walked back towards the kitchen.

"So can I ask you a question?" Christian asked.

"Shoot."

"So, it is clear that your friend, Tori, knows about you. She couldn't help hiding the fact that she knew exactly who I was and why I wanted to find out where you live. But my question is: Does anybody else know about you, except her and I?"

Eli knew exactly what Christian was asking. He was politely asking if he had come out to anybody over the years.

"Nope," he replied, "Just you and her."

"Wow," Christian responded.

"What?"

"Oh, nothing," then he said, "It just seemed that you were ready to come out way back when."

"I was," Eli admitted. "There was a good reason for coming out then."

"And what was that?" Christian questioned.

"You."

"Oh," was all the man could respond.

"You see," Eli began, "I always told myself that I would come out when I found someone that I felt comfortable enough with. I wanted to have that person standing by my side when I told the entire world the one thing I had been keeping from everyone. At one point, I thought you were going to be the one to stand by my side. Even as I was driving to see you at the walkway that final night, I had made the decision that if things worked with us, that I would do it. And I was at peace with it."

Christian didn't say anything. He was letting Eli's words sink in as he realized that he was the reason for keeping Eli from being honest with himself.

"After that night," Eli resumed, deciding not to discuss what happened four years ago again, "I didn't have a reason to do it anymore. And after awhile, it just seemed easier to do my own thing and let people assume one thing or another about me."

Once Eli finished, it was Christian's turn to ask another question. "And how do you feel about it now?"

"My thoughts on this are ever changing," Eli said. "But right now, I'm optimistic." He winked at the man in front of him.

***

Eli couldn't remember the last time that he had had so much fun. Talking with Christian over a broad range of topics over dinner was so refreshing and exciting. It reminded him of the first time that he had met the man in the parking lot of *Asian Palace*.

The two men were back in Christian's car as he drove Eli back home. Eli didn't want the night to end, but knew it would have to come to a close.

"I've had a blast tonight," he said out loud.

"It was a pretty good first date," Christian responded, smirking.

Eli responded with a smile. He loved it when Christian gave him that smirk. It drove him wild. "I don't want it to end. But I guess all good things have to eventually end."

"I wouldn't say that. You never know when you've found something that can make you happy forever."

Christian pulled up near the carport of Eli's house. He put the car into park and turned off the engine. "Let me walk you to the door."

Eli chuckled. "I'm a big boy. I think I can make it to my door."

In the flirty way that Christian was, he said, "You never know what kinda boogers are out there, waiting to prey on good looking guys like yourself."

When Eli got out of the car, Christian quickly followed. He quickly ran to Eli's side and grabbed his hand. The surge of electricity that was coursing up Eli's arm caused him to slow down his walking pace, not wanting this feeling to end.

When they reached the door, Christian leaned his hand against it, preventing Eli from opening it. "So, how many more dates do I have to take you on before you'll consider being my boyfriend?"

The question surprised Eli. He knew that Christian had feelings for him. The feeling was mutual. And he knew that their date was enjoyable for the both of them. But he had no idea that Christian was ready to take it a step further.

The question sent many different emotions clashing against each other in Eli's mind. He feared messing up the good thing that they had together. He also feared of not being a good boyfriend to Christian, since this was Eli's first real relationship, and because the standards were set by Christian's husband. But he also couldn't resist the offer that he had always hoped to get from Christian.

Eli got a little bit closer to Christian. "Who said that you had to ask me out again?"

Christian's arm made his way behind Eli's back, pulling Eli closer to him. "I'm glad to hear that, boyfriend."

Eli chuckled when he heard that word. He never thought that he and Christian would ever see each other again, let alone being in a relationship together. But here they were, making their relationship official.

Eli's eyes found Christian's, and he became immobilized. It was as if Christian had set him on stun, and had complete control of Eli. It was a nice feeling; not having to worry about the world around them. It was just the two of them.

Christian slowly leaned in closer to Eli and placed his lips on Eli's. Eli's vision instantly became blurred and his mind started to ring. Kissing Christian was unlike anything else. No other kiss that Eli had had compared to Christian's. The one kiss lasted for what seemed like forever, to Eli's pleasure.

Eli was saddened when Christian finally broke the connection, cutting Eli off from the euphoria that he was feeling. It brought Eli back to the present, which was only bearable because his source of happiness was standing in front of him. He wanted Christian to kiss him again, and if it was possible, more intensely and passionately.

"That was nice," Eli said, almost sounding drunk.

Drunk on Christian.

Christian smiled. "You certainly seemed to enjoy it."

Christian wrapped his around Eli's lower back and pulled him closer again, his chest touching Eli's. "Here's to a great beginning."

Eli was pleased to see Christian lean in for another kiss. This time, he was going to savor every second of it.

Chapter Seventeen

Eli didn't realize how one person could be responsible for someone's happiness until he began his relationship with Christian. For four weeks, Eli was constantly surprised by Christian, who would text him every morning before he woke up, as well as bringing small presents and even lunch to Eli's office.

At first, Eli was a little hesitant allowing Christian to spend so much time at his work, fearing that his co-workers would start questioning the type of relationship that he was having with the man. But once he found out how much happier he was at work, and how much productive he was, he didn't think about what anybody else thought of the new person in Eli's life.

Even Tori was aware of the change in Eli's personality. Even though she was still weary of the man, she couldn't help but admit that Christian was making Eli happy. She decided to limit the amount of insults she said in front of Eli, who would snap back at her if she dared say something about his boyfriend.

Boyfriend. Eli still couldn't get over the thought that he was now allowed to call Christian that.

"So, what do you and lover boy have planned tonight?" Tori asked as she typed an email on her computer.

Eli was sitting in a chair in front of Tori's desk, writing new appointments in his planner. "I'm not sure. Christian asked if I wanted to come over to his house tonight. He said that he had a surprise."

"How many surprises can the man give you?" A thought hit

Tori, which caused her to stop typing and turn her chair towards Eli. "You don't think it's a naked surprise, do you?"

Tori laughed hysterically as Eli threw his pen at her. He was shocked that she was insinuating that Christian's surprise was in a sexual nature.

"Get your head out of the gutter, Tori," Eli said, sitting back down and waited for Tori to return his pen to him. "Christian's not like that."

Tori shrugged her shoulders, unconvinced by what Eli was saying. "I just don't see a hunk like that staying celibate is all."

It wasn't as if the thought hadn't crossed Eli's mind. Eli was attractive in his own right, but it didn't stop him from feeling that Christian was more attractive than what Eli thought of himself.

Tori was still talking, although Eli wasn't listening to much of what she had to say. "How long are you going to make the man wait before you allow the two of you to become more intimate?"

That was also something that had passed through Eli's thoughts. Not long after their first date, Eli and Christian were laying on Eli's living room floor, playing *Sorry* when he told Christian that he was still a virgin and he was waiting for someone special. He wanted to get that out and in the open so if Christian had other thoughts, they could end things now and move on before either of them got hurt.

Instead of running away from sexual frustration, Christian put the palm of his hand on Eli's cheek and pulled him in for a tender kiss. Eli knew then and there that Christian wasn't going anywhere.

"Eli," Christian said, taking his mind off of the game. "I'm here for you in any way that you need me. I want what you want, and nothing more."

The conversation didn't come up after that, so Eli hadn't worried about it since.

"Lay off of Christian," Eli said, starting to get frustrated with her once again. "I know he hurt me. He hurt me bad. But what he has done in the last four weeks has made all those hurtful feelings wash away. Please, give him a chance."

Tori folded her arms, unable to let her guard down. "I don't know if I can," Tori said.

"Well, you're gonna have to. Because he is in my life now. And if you want to continue to be in my life, you are gonna have to live with this."

"Okay," was all that she could say, pouting like a little child.

Eli got up, needing to get back to work in his office. "I know that once you get to know him, and put the impression of him that I have forced on you over the years into the back of your mind, you'll love him." An idea came to Eli. "Hey, why don't we go on a double date together: You, me, Christian and Chris. It'll be fun."

Tori couldn't resist a night out on the town. Eli could tell that she started to lighten up with that idea in mind. "I'll think about it."

Eli walked out of her office and walked down the hall, smiling as he walked.

She'll do it.

***

Later that afternoon, Eli made his way to Christian's home, unsure what was in store for him. As always, he was more excited to see Christian than anything else in the world. But now, an un-expected dread came over him.

This would be the first time that Eli would enter Christian's home. But, he wasn't afraid of being in there. He was afraid of entering the home that Christian and Jaden had shared together. No longer was he entering just Christian's world, he was also entering Jaden's world; a ghost that he had never met before, but knew that he had existed. Memories of this man would always be in the house, which would mean he would always be with Christian.

When Eli made his way up the hill to Christian's home, he was comforted by the familiarity that he felt. After all of these years, the home still looked the same as Eli remembered it. Eli had always imagined Christian changing things as time passed, or even selling the house to buy a new one or moving in with Jaden out of town.

Over the years, Eli had been tempted by thoughts of driving back to this location to see for himself how things had changed, Christian especially. No matter how many times, or how powerful the urges were, he decided against driving nearby. He had been afraid of Christian catching him nearby and accusing him of stalking.

As he looked around the property more, Eli did notice a change beyond the perimeter of the home. He looked where Christian took him to start their journey up the mountain, a memory he remembered vividly. But the trail that had once been cleared was now overgrown with weeds and other vegetation. By the looks of it, nobody had been on the trail in years.

Eli's thoughts were interrupted when he saw Christian step out of the front door and waving towards him. Eli smiled, waved back and started unbuckling his seatbelt to start making his way towards his boyfriend.

Before Eli could make it all the way up the steps, Christian came down, blocking Eli's way. Christian put his hand on Eli's cheek, pulling him in so he could kiss him. "I'm glad you didn't get lost," Christian said, putting his forehead on Eli's. "I was afraid that you had forgotten how to get here.

"Never," Eli responded, pecking Christian on the cheek and continued up the stairs, now with Christian by his side. "I've always remembered the day we went hiking together."

That prompted a smile on Christian's face, but overall, he was more somber, more subdued than he was mere minutes ago. Had Eli said something to upset him?

Christian held the front door open so Eli could walk in. As Eli stepped inside, Christian said, "Welcome to my world."

The inside was everything that Eli had imagined that Christian's home would be. He had remodeled to give the older-looking home a much more modern look. The living room was filled with a black leather couch and a glass coffee table, both pointing towards the flat-screen TV that was mounted on the wall.

In the corner of the living room was a large desk that was covered with technological devices. Eli had always considered himself tech savvy, but even he couldn't figure out what some of the stuff was on Christian's desk. Two large computer monitors were placed in the center of the desk. It was apparent that this was Christian's most used part of the house.

"Home sweet home," Christian said behind Eli as he shut the door.

"It's very nice," Eli replied as he started to make himself comfortable and walked around the room.

"Thanks."

Eli leaned over the table of photographs near the window with a view of the forest outside. He observed the different people in Christian's life. He froze when his eyes spotted a photograph of Christian with his arms wrapped around a man who was unfamiliar to Eli. But Eli knew exactly who the man was.

Jaden.

For years, Eli had despised the man. He never knew who he was, nor did he know how Jaden was able to earn Christian's heart, but he couldn't help but feel resentment and anger towards the man.

But now, after looking at the photo of Christian and Jaden, this memory of them being so happy together, all he could feel was sympathy.

Eli finally understood why Christian fell for Jaden. The man was gorgeous. He knew that Jaden's looks wasn't the only reason for Christian pursuing him, but he could still tell. The eyes gave him away. It was as if those ocean blue eyes were a portal into the man's soul. He could tell that he had loved Christian, and that he also felt loved.

Eli didn't have to guess that the photo had been taken before Jaden's diagnosis. Even though there were no photos of him while he was sick, he could tell that Christian only wanted to remember the man that he fell in love with and married, not the man he watched waste away.

Eli didn't realize that he had picked up the photograph and was running his fingers around the frame.

Christian walked up behind Eli and noticed the frame in Eli's hands. He knew that Christian didn't mind that he was looking at it, but Eli couldn't help but feel that he was invading a part of

Christian's world that he didn't belong in.

"You both look so happy in this picture," Eli said, giving the frame to Christian when the man held his hand out for it.

Christian tried to hide his sadness with a smile. "This is my favorite photo of the two of us."

Eli couldn't keep the rush of emotions that were running through him at bay. He began to feel this old weight on his shoulders lift, a weight that Eli should have never carried. At that moment, Eli knew that Jaden and Christian had been meant for each other. And Jaden didn't steal Christian from Eli. Destiny had put the two together, and there was nothing Eli could have done about it those many years ago.

This new realization took Eli by surprise, and he could feel this wound in his soul begin to heal, and now the many unanswered questions in his head were now answered.

Eli had no problem saying what he wanted to say to Christian. "I know nothing about him, but I know without a doubt that he was a wonderful person."

Christian wrapped his arm around Eli's waist and pulled him closer. It was if Christian could read Eli's thoughts, and understood how much Eli had grown in order for him to say that. "Yes, he was."

Now that they had cleared the uncomfortable and awkward air, Eli felt that it was time to find out why he was there. "So, what is this big surprise that you brought me out here for?"

Eli could instantly feel Christian's spirit perk up once he was able to get his mind off of the past and into the present.

"Oh yeah," Christian said, letting go of Eli and walked over to the kitchen counter. "I figured since we have gone out every

Friday this month, I thought that it would be fun to stay in, watch a movie and eat junk food."

Eli didn't care what they did, as long as he got to be with Christian. "That sounds good to me. What movie did you have in mind?"

Christian came back from the kitchen with a white and blue Wal-Mart bag. He pulled out an unopened copy of *Frozen*, something that Eli was not expecting at all.

"Once upon a time," Christian said, "You promised me that we would watch this movie together. Now, it's time for you to honor that promise."

"Yes, sir," Eli responded, mocking Christian's order. "But I would have thought that you would be tired of this movie by now."

"What makes you think that?"

"Well," Eli started, "You wanted to see it so badly when it was in theatres. I can only assume that you've watched it by now."

"You assumed wrong then, because I've never watched it."

Once again, Eli was blown away by the man that he was sitting next to. Christian was able to do something as simple as buying a movie and the result was more than what Eli was prepared for. Thinking about Christian waiting to watch the movie until the day that he was able to watch it with Eli made Eli glad that he had Christian as a boyfriend.

He's unlike any person that I've ever met.

Once he put the movie in and pressed PLAY, Christian plopped on the couch, and entwined his fingers with Eli's. "So, have you seen this movie before?"

Eli decided to be truthful. "Yes. When I thought about

you a lot, I would watch it. It made me feel like you were close to me somehow."

Christian put his head on Eli's shoulder as an apologetic gesture. "Well don't you worry, because you'll have me to watch it with you now." Christian lifted his head and looked Eli in the face with a serious look. "But if you spoil anything for me, we're going to have problems."

"Okay, Disney geek."

Eli suddenly went stiff as a furry being started rubbing itself against Eli's leg. He was relieved when the familiar being jumped on the couch between Christian and Eli.

"Yoda!"

Christian chuckled. "I'm surprised that you remember him."

Eli began to pet the spotted cat as if no time had passed since seeing him. "How could I forget a cat with a name like Yoda?"

Christian started petting the cat as well. "Yoda isn't as young as he was when you first met him. He doesn't even go outside anymore."

Eli felt sorry for the poor critter and continued to pet it. Eventually, Christian grabbed Eli's hand, preventing Eli from petting Yoda any further. "If I knew that you were going to give Yoda more attention than me, I would have locked him up in my room."

Eli laughed at that and pecked Christian's cheek so that he wouldn't feel neglected any longer.

Once Yoda realized that the petting had come to an end, he jumped off of the couch and ventured into another part of the house, leaving the two men alone.

Eli had a blast while watching the movie with Christian.

He would occasionally stick his hand into the Wal-Mart bag and nibble on the candy or another prepackaged food that Christian had bought for them. When a familiar song same on, Eli would act crazy and sing as if serenading to Christian. At first, he was afraid that Christian would be aggravated, but Christian played along with Eli's flirtatious games.

Eventually, Eli got tired of putting on a show, and decided to lie next to Christian. He couldn't believe how lucky he was. He was able to feel each breath that Christian took, each beat that his heart made, and he was able to smell the wonderful smell that radiated off of the man. He cared so much for the man that his desire for Christian grew more intense. There was nothing more that he wanted than to explore the depths of their relationship. But he knew that he wasn't ready to go down that road with Christian, and he wasn't sure that Christian was ready either.

When the movie ended, Christian stretched, reaching for the ceiling, and then wrapped his arms around Eli. "I can't believe I waited four years to see that."

Eli shook his head. "Before you know it, you'll be singing *Let It Go* until you get sick." He got up and walked over to the window. It was so dark outside, Eli was no longer able to see the growed up trail beyond Christian's property.

"Are you leaving?" Christian asked, stretching himself out on the sofa as he watched Eli gather his things.

"Yeah," Eli responded, rubbing his stomach. "I shouldn't have taken up your idea on eating junk food. I'm gonna be up on night."

Christian got off of the couch and got close to Eli, putting his hands in Eli's. "You know, when you feel like it, you're always

The One

welcome to stay here."

Eli wasn't sure how far the invitation went, but Eli did know that it was Christian's way of saying that he felt comfortable around him, and that allowing Eli to come and go in his house hadn't been done since Jaden's death. The gesture overwhelmed Eli with happiness.

"Thank you," Eli said, kissing Christian tenderly on the lips. "That means a lot."

Christian walked Eli outside to his car. Eli didn't want the night to end. He felt like every second with his boyfriend went by too fast.

"So, I've been talking with Tori, and I think that I've got her warmed up to going on a double date with us. What do you think of that?"

Christian looked unsure, but said, "I'm fine with that. But are you?"

That was a question that Eli had also asked himself. Tori's fiancé, Chris, didn't know that Eli was attracted to both sexes. It was something that Eli made Tori promise that she wouldn't tell the man. He hadn't been around Chris much, but he did respect him, and knew that he would make Tori a great husband. But was he comfortable enough sharing a side of himself with the man that only Tori and Christian knew up to this point?

"I am," Eli finally said. "I know, Tori's fiancée would make one more person that knows about me, and I'm sorta okay with it. As long as you're with me, I'm not afraid."

"Good," Christian said, leaning in for another kiss, "Because I'm not going anywhere."

207

Chapter Eighteen

Several weeks passed before Eli was able to schedule the double date with Tori. She had been busy getting the beginning of the school year started with Dr. Roslin. Eli didn't mind. He was glad that he was able to put off the awkward conversation with her.

"What's up?" She said as Eli entered the office.

"I was hoping I could talk to you about something."

"Okay," she responded with suspicion in her voice.

Eli knew that he could tell his best friend anything. She was the first person that he told about his sexuality. Talking to her about coming out to Chris was no different.

"You remember me suggesting that you, Christian, Chris and I should go on a double date?"

"Yeah…"

"Well," Eli resumed, ripping the imaginary band-aid off, one millimeter at a time. "I took the idea to Christian, and he likes it. He's really looking forward to getting to know you and Chris."

Tori smiled, her suspicion gone from her face. "I think that's a great idea."

Hearing her say those words took Eli by surprise. "You do?"

"Yeah," she said. "You were right, Eli, I didn't give Christian a fair chance after he came back into your life. Or the weeks following that. But I see how he makes you feel, and I can't be mad at him for that. So I think it's time that I got to know my best friend's boyfriend better."

Hearing that come from Tori warmed Eli's heart. She was

really making an effort for him. He gave her a big smile and said, "Thanks, Tori. I really appreciate it."

The two of them smiled for a moment before Eli remembered why he actually came to talk to her.

"There's something else I need to talk to you about."

"Okay, go ahead," she said, turning around to grab a folder.

"I need to come out to Chris."

That immediately turned Tori around, with her jaw dropped. "You have to come out to Chris? Why?"

"Because," Eli said, trying to lay it all out with his hand gestures, "When I'm around Christian, I don't want to hide who I am. And if we go out with you two, I don't want us to pretend we are something that we're not. I don't know how he'll react, but I think it is best that we clear the elephant out of the room before Chris makes his own assumptions."

Tori started laughing hysterically, resulting in Eli being confused. He didn't know why she was laughing. It was a serious issue for him.

"What's your problem?" Eli asked.

Tori tried to show that she was okay by waving her hands. When she could finally speak she said, "I don't think you need to do that."

"Why's that?"

"Because he knows about you," Tori said.

At first, Eli could feel his insides burning. The thought that Tori betraying his trust and telling Chris without Eli's permission was unforgiveable. Then he felt a wave of relief, glad that he no longer had to deal with the issue. Then the anger started to return.

"He knows?" Eli said with a loud voice. "How? Why? Why would you tell him?"

Tori immediately went on the defensive. "Who said that I told him? I would never tell anybody something that you didn't want me to disclose."

Eli didn't understand. "Then how does he know?"

Tori sighed, walked over next to her friend, and put her hand on his shoulders. "Honey, he figured it out all on his own."

Eli still didn't understand how Chris could have figured it out by himself. Eli had tried to be very careful keeping his secret hidden. "How?"

"Because you're you," Tori said. "Just because you don't want people to know the truth about you, doesn't mean that people can't figure it out for themselves. He came to me one night after you were at the house, and he was like 'Eli likes guys, doesn't he?' At that point, I didn't see the point in keeping it from him."

Eli let what his friend said sink in. Apparently he was more obvious with his feelings than he thought. "What does he think of me now?"

Tori shook her head, realizing that Eli still wasn't getting her point. "He still thinks the world of you. Just because he knows that you bat for both teams, doesn't mean that you're not still Eli. Once he knew the truth, he didn't blow up or say that he didn't want you around me anymore. He did say, however, that you were doing yourself an injustice by not being honest with the people around you, or yourself."

This was not the reaction that Eli had hoped for. He thought that they would have a heated debate on whether to tell Chris his secret. But it seemed like Eli's secret wasn't so much a secret. But still, he treated it like it was.

After a few minutes of processing all that Tori said, calmness came over him. Yes, Tori and Chris were both right. He shouldn't have to hide from the truth, or keep it from anybody else. All he could think about, though, was that he no longer had to worry about the four of them acting awkward during their double date. Whenever it came to Christian, Eli didn't care what people thought of him.

"Well," Eli finally responded. At this point, Tori had resumed her work at her desk. When he spoke up, she returned her attention to him. "I guess all we have to worry about now is when we want to go out."

Tori smiled, realizing that she had gotten through to Eli on some level. "How about this Thursday? I am slammed on Friday and won't be able to focus on anything else but work."

"It's a date," Eli replied.

***

The music was blaring in Eli's car as he was driving to Christian's house. He told his boyfriend that since Christian had taken him out so many times, that it was Eli's turn to take him out. Christian resisted for days, but eventually gave in when it sunk in that Eli wasn't going to give up any time soon.

Eli was super excited about the night ahead of them. He made the extra effort to look nice for Christian. He went and gotten his hair cut and bought a solid black button-down shirt. To Eli, black was the sexiest color, and he wanted to look his best when he finally had the chance to show Christian off.

He pulled into the driveway and rushed to the front door, eager to see the man inside. Lately, it was as if Eli could barely think if he wasn't around Christian. No other person had made him feel the way he felt now, and he wasn't sure if there was another person in the world that could make him feel this way. He didn't want to say the L word, because the last time he did, Christian walked out of his life. He didn't want that to happen again. But, he had to admit that what they had was genuine.

After a few knocks on the door, Christian was there, all ready to go. Eli couldn't hold it in any longer, throwing his arms around Christian and kissing him with all of his might. The kiss was good, but Eli could almost detect Christian pulling away. It was something odd for his boyfriend, which set fear deep into Eli's soul.

"Hey babe," Eli said after he broke their kiss. "Are you okay?"

"Oh yeah," Christian said nonchalantly. "Long day at work. I'm just tired."

Eli didn't believe Christian, but he didn't want to press the issue. If Christian said that he was fine, he would take the man at his word and move on. "Okay, are you ready to go?"

"You bet," Christian said, smiling.

Eli smiled back. Christian was totally off, but he guessed that if his boyfriend wanted him to know what was wrong, he would tell him.

He looked over Christian's shoulder, spotting Yoda inside, laying on the couch. "You be a good boy, okay?"

Christian chuckled as he watched Eli talking to the cat.

Maybe he's fine after all?

As they walked to the car together, Eli couldn't help but ask a question. "Christian?"

"Hmm?"

"Do you still go hiking?" Eli asked, putting his arms on the hood of the car.

Christian looked surprise by the question. "Why do you ask?"

Eli gestured towards the former trail that lied in the visible forest. "It's just that I noticed that the trail is grown up."

"Yeah," was all that Christian could say. He took a sigh, and said, "Once Jaden got sick, I wasn't able to do it anymore. And after—" He stopped himself, then said, "Afterwards, I lost all interest in it."

Christian didn't say anything. Instead he got in the car and waited for Eli to follow him.

Christian was pretty quiet during their drive to meet Tori and Chris. If anything was said between the two of them, it was because Eli initiated the conversation. This was unlike Christian. Christian always had something to say, or as a last result, he would flirt. Christian was a hard worker, but Eli never saw him so tired that he wasn't his usual self.

Eli pulled into the parking lot of *Roadhouse Bar and Grill,* a restaurant that was attached to the *Arcade Hut* arcade center. Eli and Tori agreed that they would never go back to the place, but they couldn't deny that the food that the *Roadhouse* served was beyond irresistible.

They parked right next to Tori's car, where Tori and Chris waited inside. As soon as they saw Eli and Christian pull up next to them, they started getting out of the car.

Eli looked over at Christian, who looked zoned out. "You ready?"

After a second, Christian looked over at Eli, smiled and nodded.

"Yay, you're here," Tori said. "I thought you would never make it."

Chris, a muscular, attractive man, walked next to her and wrapped his arm over her shoulder. "Thank God you made it here, Eli. I didn't think I could stay in the car with her any longer." The comment resulted in an elbow in the gut, courtesy of Tori.

Once Chris recovered, Eli walked over to him with his hand held out. "It's good to see you again, Chris."

"And you too, Eli. "

Tori made sounds as if she was trying to clear her throat. "Uh, Eli. Are you going to introduce us?"

Eli turned his head to see Christian get out of the car. As Christian walked closer to him, Eli wrapped his arm around his waist. He figured the gesture would speak volumes to Tori and Chris. "Guys, this is Christian."

Christian walked towards Tori, breaking Eli's grip, and kissed her lightly on the cheek. "It's a pleasure to officially meet you."

"Same to you," Tori said, getting red in the face.

Christian then held out his hand towards Chris. "It's nice to meet you as well, Chris."

"Likewise," Chris said. Then he smiled and said, "Have you been able to keep Eli in line?"

Everybody laughed at the joke. Once they all calmed down, Christian was able to say, "I try."

The four of them started walking towards the entrance of the restaurant. Tori started walking slower, eventually walking next to Eli as the other two men walked ahead.

"God, he's gorgeous," Tori said. "If he wasn't gay, and in a relationship with you, I'd be all over that."

"Watch it," Eli said nodding his head towards Chris. "Don't let your fiancé hear you say that."

"He knows he's my one and only," Tori said. "So it doesn't hurt to fanaticize."

Eli responded with a smile, but didn't laugh at the joke. He was looking at Christian and still detected sadness in the man's face. He knew that something wasn't right.

"What's wrong?" Tori asked, slowing her pace even more so the men ahead of them were out of earshot.

"Nothing," Eli said at first, but knew that he couldn't keep anything from Tori for long. "I'm worried about Christian. He's not himself today."

"Some people have off days," Tori said. "Now that you're in a relationship, you'll have to realize that sometimes people need their space."

Eli would have agreed with that, except this was beyond what Eli would consider an "off day" for Christian.

He could only hope that Christian held it together as they walked inside the restaurant.

***

The four were eating their meal, with mainly Eli and Tori leading the conversation. They talked about their jobs and the different strategies Dr. Roslin had presented to Tori.

"He's going to ask you to start going to the radio station every day, instead of once a week to go on the air and talk about school-related stuff. I tried to talk him out of it, but he is insistent that it's a good idea to keep the school system in the back of people's minds."

Eli took a sip of his drink before he responded. "As long as I get paid, I don't care. How many people can say that they get paid to talk on the radio and represent their company?"

Tori continued to rattle on, and occasionally, she turned her head to get a response from Chris, who was focusing more on his food and alcoholic beverage than her.

Eli looked over at Christian. The man had been quiet throughout dinner. He would only talk when Tori or Chris would ask him a direct question. Other than that, there was nothing. Something was going on inside the man's head, and it was killing Eli to see this vibrant man so miserable.

It wasn't long after Tori finished her stories about her job when she started again. "So what if we went and saw a movie tonight?"

That appeared to be a breaking point for Christian. Before any of them could answer, Christian said "Excuse me," shot up out of his chair and rushed off to the restroom.

Eli made a sigh of sadness and looked over at Tori, who's eyes were big.

"Okay," Tori said, admitting defeat, "Maybe something is wrong with him."

"Duh," Eli responded, mocking the woman in front of him which made Chris laugh. "He was fine yesterday. So I have no idea what could be wrong."

"Usually," Chris popped up, finishing his bite of steak, "If Tori ran off to the bathroom like that, it was because I did something wrong. And I would just sit here and finish my dinner." His comment received a nasty glare from Tori. But he continued, "But it's clear that Christian cares about you. So in that case, I think you should go after him and see what's wrong."

"You're right," Eli said, glad that someone thought that he should investigate what was wrong with Christian. He pushed his seat back and went in the direction of the bathroom.

As soon as he stepped inside, he saw Christian leaned over the bathroom sink, his eyes red and puffy from crying. Once he saw Eli's reflection in the mirror, Christian tried to contain himself, but a few sobs managed to escape.

"Christian, what's wrong?" Eli put a hand on Christian's shoulder and waited for the man to respond.

"I need to go home," was all that Christian would say.

"Are you sick? Do you not like Tori and Chris? I shouldn't have pushed you to meet them."

"No, they're great. I...I just need to go home."

Eli nodded his head, ready to obey Christian's request. "Okay. You go on outside and I'll tell Tori and Chris that we're leaving."

Christian nodded his head. A few more sobs escaped as he walked out the door. The man was a mess.

Christian was no better by the time Eli reached the car, or during the car ride. To help make things less awkward, Eli played some music in the background so Christian could sob freely without having to worry about what Eli thought.

Eli racked his brain to try and figure out what could be bothering Christian. He said that he liked Tori and Chris, so it wasn't that. Maybe someone in Christian's family was sick. But the last Christian said, everybody was fine. Maybe he had been fired from his job?

Then a sinking feeling hit Eli.

Maybe it has something to do with me?

Eli couldn't think how it could be about him, but he couldn't help but let the worry wash over him. Maybe Christian didn't think he could go on dating Eli, and the thought of having to break up was very upsetting.

He tried to push those thoughts out of his mind and think positively. Instead of finding out what was wrong with his boyfriend, like he originally intended on doing, he planned to just drop Christian off at his house, preventing him from breaking Eli's heart again.

They reached Christian's home. Usually, Eli was so excited to be here. But now, he couldn't wait to leave. The longer he stayed there, the better a chance there was that Christian would make Eli's worst fears come true again.

Instead of pushing Christian out of the car and driving away, he got out with Christian and walked the man to the door. Once Christian unlocked the door and went inside, Eli turned around and started walking down the stairs. "I'll talk to you later."

"Wait."

Eli turned around and looked at the broken man before him. "I thought I would leave you alone and let you work out whatever is going on with you."

"Please," Christian said, holding the door open for Eli. "Stay with me."

The fact that Christian wanted Eli with him made Eli think that none of this was about him. So in that case, Eli wanted to be there for his boyfriend for whatever was causing him to be so upset.

He went inside and sat on the couch next to Christian. Once he sat, Christian laid his head down on Eli's lap and stayed there for a long time. Eli didn't say anything. He figured that when Christian was ready to tell him what it was, he would. So instead, he rubbed his fingers through Christian's hair as a sign that he was there for Christian, no matter what.

"Jaden died on this day."

Eli could feel his pants getting wet from Christian's tears. Hearing Christian speak those words made sense of everything for Eli. He never thought to think about the anniversary of Jaden's death.

"Oh God," Eli said, kissing Christian's head. "I am so sorry. I never should have suggested that we go out tonight."

"You didn't know."

"Yeah," Eli said, "but I should have known the moment I saw you this afternoon that you weren't in any shape to do anything."

"I really wanted to go," Christian said, taking several gasping breaths. "You were so excited about introducing me to your friends. And I knew that this was a big step for you. But eventually, it got too much for me. I didn't want to make a big scene and embarrass you."

Eli's heart felt like it was breaking. Seeing Christian so hurt was too much to bear. It was as if Christian's pain was spreading, hoping to latch on to anything else that had emotion.

Tears started to swell in Eli's eyes. "You could never do that."

He wished he could do something, anything for the man who had his head in Eli's lap. Even if that meant bringing back Christian's lost love. Even if that meant never being with Christian again. The realization hit Eli that he loved Christian with all of his heart. So much, that he was willing to sacrifice his own happiness to make the one he loved happy. It was something that he had never felt before, something that no other person could give him in this life.

Eli wiped the tears away from his eyes and continued to brush his hands through Christian's hair. "Just let it out, Christian. And I'll be here for you the entire way."

The two men cried with each other until they fell into the darkness of sleep.

***

Eli had no idea how long he had been asleep when he woke up. For a few moments, he was disoriented and unaware of where he was. Eventually, he realized that he was at Christian's house, on Christian's couch. His head dropped down to see Christian's head on his lap, but didn't see the man who was there hours ago.

"Morning," Christian said, sitting beside Eli with his legs crossed Indian-style.

Eli yawned and wiped his eyes, trying to wake up. "How long have you been up?"

"Several hours," Christian responded. "Couldn't sleep."

Eli looked around the living room and noticed that neither the TV, nor the computers were on. "What have you been doing then?"

"Watching you sleep."

It sounded creepy, but Eli couldn't help but find it sweet. He chuckled and said, "I bet that was exciting."

"Yeah," Christian said. "It gave me time to think."

"Think about what?"

"You. Me. Us. I was watching you sleep and I couldn't help thinking that you were willing to stay with me, to cry with me until

I felt better. Even though I was hurting over the loss of my dead husband."

"That's what a good boyfriend does," Eli smiled. "We stand by the ones we care about, no matter what the case may be."

"You're more than a good boyfriend. You are so much more, I can't even describe what you are. And I love you for that." Christian realized what he had said, causing both of their eyes to grow large. Then Christian smiled and said, "I love you."

Eli could feel his heart ready to beat out of his chest. This was something that he had always dreamed that would happen. Now it had become a reality. He barely knew what to do. So he did the only thing that made sense.

He put his hands on Christian's face and said, "I love you too. More than you know."

Their lips came together like magnets. The kiss was more than Eli could handle. But he wanted to take it all in, and more. Hearing that Christian reciprocated Eli's feelings made him feel more inside his soul than anything else in the world. To remove these feelings would be just as bad as if someone was to stab Eli right in the heart.

"I hope I can make you happy," Eli said after they broke the kiss.

"You already have."

They returned to kissing, expressing their love towards each other as the sun started to peek through the forest, the windows and into Christian's home.

Chapter Nineteen

It had been a month and a half since Eli and Christian said that they loved each other. And after that morning, Eli's life changed. He had spent more time with Christian in public, he had Tori and Chris over to his house while Christian was there, and he started staying over at Christian's house some nights, sleeping on the couch of course. He was madly in love, and he was enjoying every minute of it.

"Tonight, the JV football team will be competing against our rival over in Sylva. We wish our players luck in their game," Eli said into the microphone in front of him.

As Tori predicted, Dr. Roslin came to Eli with the idea of visiting the radio station every day to keep the public informed on daily events. Eli didn't mind it much, but the constant trips into town for a few minutes started to aggravate him.

"This is Eli Cooper with Forrester County Schools, wishing you and your families a great day."

"Thank you, Eli," said Randy, the radio host, "Now let's go to Isaac for the weather report."

Eli grabbed his backpack lying on the chair behind him and walked out of the studio room. When nobody was around to talk to, like there usually was, he went outside to his car.

When he felt his phone ring in his pants pocket, he pulled it out and noticed that it was Christian.

"Hello?"

"Hey babe."

Eli smiled. Ever since they took their relationship to a deeper level, Christian would tease Eli by calling him "babe." If Christian was in front of him, he would have punched him in the shoulder.

"What are you doing today?"

"Listening to you on the radio, actually. Made me think of you."

Eli got this kind of call from Christian every time he got out of the station. "You don't sound like a stalker at all."

"You know you love it," Christian said. "So I was thinking that we could do something tonight."

"Sure," Eli said, happy with that idea. "What are you thinking?"

"I don't know," Christian said, "But I wanted to do something outside since it's such a nice day. Maybe go walking on the walkway or something."

An idea hit Eli, and he was so excited by it, he could hardly think.

"How about we meet at your house when you get off work, and we'll decide then."

"Sounds like a plan," Christian said. "I better get back to work. I love you."

Eli never got tired of hearing the man say that. "I love you too. Bye."

He disconnected the call before Christian could possibly say something back. He immediately started dialing his phone again.

"Forrester County Board of Education, this is Caroline."

"Hi, Caroline," Eli said, unlocking his car and getting inside. "This is Eli. I just wanted to let you know that I'm taking the rest of the day off."

"Okay," Caroline said, sounding concerned. "Are you okay?"

"Yes, I'm fine. Just going to take a personal day."

Eli talked with the receptionist a little bit longer before he hung up and put the car into reverse.

The idea in his head caused his heart to race with anticipation. He couldn't wait to show Christian what he had in store for him.

***

Eli was waiting at Christian's house for his boyfriend to return home from work. He used the key that Christian had given him to get inside, take a shower and lay on the couch.

He was exhausted from executing his plan, but he knew that it was worth it. And he couldn't wait to see the look on Christian's face when he realized what Eli had done with his day off.

Yoda was lying on top of him, and Eli was petting the cat lightly on the top of his head when they both heard Christian's electric car start ascending up the hill.

Both Eli and Yoda were waiting at the top of the stairs as they waited for Christian to park the car in front of the driveway.

Christian was surprised to see Eli waiting for him. "What are you doing here so early? I thought that you would just now be leaving work."

"I took the day off," Eli responded while stepping down and reaching for Christian's hands.

Christian looked confused. "Why did you take the day off?"

"Because," Eli said, motioning toward the forest that was behind Christian, "I wanted to surprise you."

It took Christian a moment to realize what Eli meant. But

seeing the weed eater and the can of gasoline sitting nearby made Christian look a little bit closer.

Before him was the trail that he had made so many years ago. But instead of the grown up trail, it was cleared, all of the years of neglect removed from sight.

"You cleared the trail!" Christian exclaimed with surprise in his voice.

"You said that you wanted to do something outside this evening."

Christian walked up to Eli and kissed him passionately on the lips to show his gratitude.

And Eli gratefully accepted.

"You are amazing," Christian said after catching his breath.

"I try," Eli teased, glad that he got the reaction from Christian that he had wanted.

Christian took a step back and observed Eli's look. "You look too good for someone that has been working outside all day."

"I had to shower, I was so filthy." Eli pushed Christian jokingly. "You really let that trail grow out of control."

Christian shook his head in agreement and said, "Well, let's go and see what all you did. I'll run and grab my boots."

Eli watched as Christian ran up the stairs and into the house. He was give out and exhausted, but he was hoping that Christian would suggest hiking up the trail. He had a few more surprises in store for Christian.

By the time that Christian had made his way back outside, Eli had slipped on his own boots and waited at the edge of the forest.

"Come on, let's go," Christian said, grabbing Eli's hand,

leading him up the trail.

***

At the end of the trail, Christian was huffing and puffing.

"I had no idea how much of a workout it was to walk up here."

"Oh, stop your complaining," Eli countered back. "I've walked up here twice today."

"Poor baby," Christian said, grabbing Eli into an embrace.

They walked closer to the edge of the trail to admire the beauty that was before them.

The sun was starting to set, the lights of Pinecrest starting to come on and bouncing the light off of the mountains.

"I guess we better head back before it gets dark." Christian started to turn back to the trail.

Eli grabbed Christian's arm, preventing him from going any further. "Hold on. Who said that I was done with my surprise?"

"There's more?"

Eli smiled. "Oh yeah."

Eli entwined his fingers with his boyfriend's and led him to the other clearing that Eli made.

Before them was a blanket and several pillows. Eli knew exactly what they were for, but it appeared that Christian didn't.

Christian's thoughts went south, which caused a large grin to appear on his face. He started chuckling before saying, "What exactly did you bring me up here for?"

Eli looked back at it and knew what Christian was thinking. He elbowed his boyfriend in the ribs. "Not that kind of surprise, I'm afraid." Christian was still chuckling. "You dirty boy. I thought we could lay here and look at the stars and talk."

Understanding Eli's true intentions, Christian grabbed him and threw both of them on top of the blanket. "Sounds good to me." Christian looked around. "I'm surprise that you didn't light candles or anything."

The thought certainly had crossed Eli's mind. "Well, I wanted to, but I was afraid that I would burn this side of the mountain down. I didn't want to be arrested for arson."

Christian rolled on top of Eli, pinning him down and unable to move. "It was a sweet gesture, nevertheless."

The two men kissed. It couldn't have been a more intimate setting for Eli. Everything today was going as he had hoped for. In fact, the entire relationship with Christian was going exactly as he had always imagined it. Except now, it was a reality.

The sun had long disappeared when the couple continued their stories and discussions. What felt like mere minutes was actually hours.

"So let me ask you something," Christian said.

"Go ahead," Eli responded, propping his head up with his hand.

Christian got close, close enough for Eli to feel the man's breath. To kiss him. "Tell me your dreams for the future."

Eli wasn't expecting this request. He thought he was going to ask something about not coming out or even his past experiences with other men and women. But he had no idea that Christian would ask this.

"You really wanna know?"

"So badly, it hurts," Christian said softly.

Eli couldn't deny his boyfriends request. "I want to get

married. The whole tradition and being attracted to men didn't seem like a reality for me. And as much as I thought that I didn't want kids, I want them. Not a whole lot, but enough to pass on what I have learned and make them better than I am. And above all, I want to be honest with my family. Because as long as I'm not honest with them, I'm not honest with myself."

Christian nodded his head. "And does your future include me in it?"

Eli didn't have to wait for the answer to enter his thoughts. He already knew. "Yes, it does."

Christian nodded his head, but didn't say anything, which prompted Eli to ask Christian what his thoughts were.

"Do you see yourself in my future?" The question made Eli feel like he was playing a game with death. The answer would either keep him alive, or he would die from it.

Christian looked Eli directly in the eyes when he said, "Yes, I do."

The response from his boyfriend made Eli relax. He was glad that Christian felt the same way. But he couldn't help but ask so many more questions. Was Christian bringing up the topic of marriage? The thought was too much for Eli to process.

"What do you want your future to look like?"

Christian looked at Eli, contemplating his response before speaking. "After Jaden died, I didn't think that my future mattered. I existed, but I wasn't living. And any dreams that I had for myself were bleak."

Hearing those things broke Eli's heart. He didn't want to hear how Christian was so broken.

"But then I met you," Christian said.

That instantly lifted Eli's spirits. Every time Christian told him that he was the one who helped him escape his depressing abyss, it made him feel special, like a superhero even.

"Finding you and being with you has made me feel in ways that I didn't think I could feel again. You are my future, Eli, and any dreams that I have are the dreams that I hope you'll share with me."

Eli wasn't prepared for the deep thoughts that Christian had just confessed to him. Knowing these things showed Eli just how much Christian loved him. Eli had always thought that he had cared for Christian more than Christian had cared for him. But that didn't seem to be the case.

Eli put his hand on the back of Christian's head and pulled him in for a kiss. He loved Christian so much that kissing him, touching him just wasn't enough. He couldn't get enough of the man.

"I love you. More than you know," Eli said after breaking the kiss.

"I know," Christian said back. "But I love you more."

Eli didn't have time to process Christian's sweet response before Christian spoke up again.

"I want you to meet my mom."

Eli had wondered if they would ever come to this point. Never in his life had he gotten close and comfortable enough with somebody to meet their parents. It was something that Eli knew that it was a big deal, but never had the pleasure of being asked.

"You're serious?"

"Yeah," Christian responded. "I thought that we could go down Friday evening after work, and come back on Sunday."

"Okay," Eli said, sounding unsure of himself.

Christian could tell why Eli was hesitant. "She'll love you. I know that you're not ready to tell the rest of the world about you. But my mother is very accepting. She didn't judge me when I came out to her, and she liked Jaden when she met him for the first time. And I know that the same thing is going to happen with you."

Eli was instantly reminded of what Christian had written on the equality forum.

She kept commenting on how much more I smile and laugh and said that when I talk about him, my voice takes a much softer tone.

Would she say the same thing about Eli?

He knew that he would dread it, but he didn't want to turn Christian down. He knew that it meant so much to his boyfriend.

"Okay."

Christian kissed Eli with happiness. "I'm so excited. You're going to love her."

Eli wanted to agree with him, but couldn't help but think that the standards that Jaden had set were lingering over his head.

Ready to head back down the mountain, Eli nudged Christian in his side. Christian didn't respond, quickly falling into the abyss of sleep.

Even though this wasn't part of the surprise, Eli wrapped his arms around Christian's body, feeling his warmth, and bracing for the unknown which was ahead of them.

Chapter Twenty

To Eli's displeasure, the time to visit Christian's family had arrived. As the day of their trip approached, the more hesitant that Eli was about going. But seeing Christian so happy about visiting his mother silenced any motivation to tell Christian that he didn't want to go.

After they both got off work, the couple met at Eli's house, where they packed their things in Eli's car. By that time, Eli was done resisting it: He was going whether he wanted to or not.

As they made their way on their adventure, Christian could tell that Eli was not looking forward to what lied in store for them at their destination. "Relax, Eli. My mom and step-dad are going to love you."

"Sure," Eli sarcastically said. "That's what they always say in the movies, right before the parents show their true selves."

Christian shook his head. "My parents are not like that. That's why I had no problem telling them about me years ago. It was certainly easier with them than with my dad and step-mother."

Hearing that gave Eli more to look forward to in the future.

Eli didn't want to sound mean, but he had to be truthful to his boyfriend, who was more optimistic than he was himself. "Christian, just because they liked Jaden, doesn't mean that they won't like me."

He hadn't meant for it to sting, but he could see it on Christian's face. Hurting Christian was the last thing that he ever wanted to do.

"That may be true," Christian conceded, "But I've told them how much I love you. So if they don't feel the same way, it's their loss."

Eli was speechless. "You've told them that you love me?"

"Yes, sir."

Eli had no idea how freely Christian spoke with his parents. He was completely honest with them and they returned the same to him, without judgment or prejudice. It was a relationship that Eli had always wished for him and his family.

An easiness overcame Eli. Christian wasn't worried in the least about what his parents would think about Eli. So why should he? He had to trust Christian and believe that everything would work out.

Eli laid his hand on Christian's knee, realizing exactly what he had said earlier. "I'm sorry about what I said. It was uncalled for."

Christian laid his hand on top of Eli's and squeezed it lovingly. "You're concerns are valid. And I know that you didn't bring Jaden up in a derogatory way. But my marriage to Jaden and his relationship with my parents will not predetermine how they will respond to you. You're not 'the other man'. So please, let my parents get to know you and love you the same way that I do."

Now that the troubled waters had been calmed, Eli felt well enough to joke with Christian. "Are you sure you want them to love me the same way you do?"

They both laughed, allowing any remaining tension to escape on the road behind them.

Eli was finally looking forward to exploring the other part of Christian's world.

***

The sun had set many hours before they arrived in Savannah, Georgia. Eli had only visited the area once, but enjoyed visiting the unique houses along the shoreline. It was unlike any other beaches that Eli had been to. This area was more of a residency rather than a commercial hotspot. It was a nice change.

"My mom is a fabulous cook," Christian spoke up. "I always look forward to her cooking. And knowing Johnny, we'll probably be having seafood tonight."

"What makes you say that?"

"When he's not working, he's fishing," Christian said, looking out towards the endless sea. "I'm hoping that he'll be interested in going out and fishing sometime while we're here."

Eli was glad that Christian thought of his step-father as a father figure. Hearing the stories about his real father, he could understand why he wasn't introducing Eli to him first. He wondered if his relationship with his own father would change when and if he was as honest as Christian was with his family.

Christian indicated which house to turn to a few meters before arriving. Eli was in awe once they pulled up next to the house.

The house looked like a real-life sand castle. The stucco walls were painted a tan color, with Mexican roofing painted a dark red. It was certainly a house that you wouldn't see in the Appalachian Mountains. Eli was surprised that Christian had never entertained the thought of moving down here with his mother. It looked like Johnny and Christian's mother lived rather comfortably.

"Uh, what does your step-father do for a living?" Eli asked, still trying to absorb all of the details of the house. He drove through the gate that was open for their expected arrival.

"An accountant," Christian replied. "He's hoping that he can retire in a few years and just go fishing every day for fun."

"Well, with the money I'm sure he's making, I wouldn't give it up too soon."

Eli parked his Civic Hybrid in front of the double door garage. He got out and couldn't help but admire the cobblestone driveway that his feet rested on.

"I had no idea that you had such good taste," Christian said, raising the hatchback of the car and noticing Eli's admiration.

"Neither did I," Eli responded.

The front door of the house opened, with two people the age of Eli's parents, stepping out and walking towards them.

"My baby!" The woman squealed as she ran to hug her son.

"Hi, mom," Christian gasped as his mother ran into him. Once he caught his breath, he embraced her in a big hug.

As Christian and his mother savored in their reunion, the man presumed as Johnny stepped next to Eli and held his hand out. He wasn't near as muscular as Christian, but it looked as though that the man got his daily activity in. His age was starting to show, his hair graying on the top of his head.

"Nice to meet you, son," Johnny said as Eli took his hand and shook it. "We've heard so much about you."

Eli could only imagine what Christian had told them. He just smiled and turned his attention back to Christian.

Once the mother and her child disconnected, Christian remembered Eli. He motioned his mother in Eli and Johnny's direction. "Mom, this is Eli. Eli, this is my mother, Shelly."

Eli held his hand out to shake her hand, but was instead

invaded by a big hug, despite the small woman that was wrapped around him.

"It is so nice to meet you, Eli," she said, finally allowing him air. "I've been waiting to see you for some time."

"Likewise," Eli lied. Even though he already felt welcomed by Christian's parents, he couldn't help but remember the hesitant feelings that he felt before making the journey to visit them. He winked at Christian, who knew he wasn't quite as honest with his answer.

"Come on inside," Shelly said, ushering the two of them in the house. "Dinner is just about finished."

Eli was in awe when he stepped into the foyer of the house. The high ceilings sparkled from the light that shown off of the crystal chandelier. Christian had to move him to keep him from being mesmerized.

Christian took Eli to the dining room, where the table was already set and awaiting the food. Christian took him to a corner of the room and whispered so nobody in the house could hear. "What do you think?"

"They're wonderful. Your mom can't get enough of you."

"I get that a lot from people," Christian teased, implying the same about Eli.

Eli rolled his eyes and took a seat as Shelly and Johnny brought in several dishes.

In front of him was an island of seafood. Crab legs, shrimp, scallops and fish. His stomach rumbled from desire to eat the delicious food. He had to restrain himself, though. He didn't want to look barbaric in front of Christian's family.

"Dig in," Shelly said as she sat down and put the cloth napkin in her lap.

As Christian and Johnny started passing the food around, Eli couldn't help but observe all of the work that was put into the meal. "You cooked all of this, Shelly?"

"Well, I can't take all of the credit. Johnny here did catch a lot of this."

Johnny nodded, pleased to have contributed to Shelly's meal.

Eli smiled at Shelly as he grabbed a bowl of scallops from Christian. "It's wonderful. Thank you."

"Anything for my son," Shelly said, smiling at Christian from across the table.

After Shelly and Johnny got a chance to catch up with Christian a little bit, Shelly returned her attention to Eli. "So Christian tells us that you work for the school system."

Eli wiped his napkin across his mouth before he spoke. "Yes, I'm the public relations director."

"Well, I sure hope that the system has gotten better since Christian left. Poor baby, he never stood a chance over there."

Eli was reminded of the boy who was humiliated in front of their entire class. It was amazing how far they had both come and changed over the many years. Eli could only imagine how Shelly acted towards her life's treasure when she saw him in such misery.

Eli resumed to his dinner when Shelly asked him another question.

"So, is Christian your first boyfriend, Eli?"

"Mom," Christian protested, but Eli stopped him before he could say anymore. It was the one thing that he had dreaded talking about with Christian's family. But he knew that Christian had told them everything, so the chances of them bringing it up were good. Why else would their son want to bring someone all the way between states to introduce him to them?

As much as he resisted coming down here to face this exact question, being around Shelly, Johnny and Christian made him feel comfortable and free of judgment. He knew that he didn't have anything to worry about.

"Yes, he is," Eli said, putting his hand on Christian's leg.

Shelly smiled at the two of them. She asked, "And have your parents met him yet?" before taking a bite of her food.

Eli shook his head with shame. "No, they haven't. They don't know about us. They don't even know that I am attracted to both sexes."

Shelly and Johnny nodded with understanding. They didn't look shocked by this news, which meant that Christian had told them *everything* after all.

Johnny spoke up then. "And do you plan on telling them soon?"

Christian leaned in to hear the answer to his step-father's question. He was as eager to hear Eli's response as his parents were. Maybe he even put Johnny up to asking the question.

"That's a good question," Eli said. "To be honest, I haven't thought about it a whole lot. I know that it's something that I should be thinking about, but when I'm around Christian, every worry just sort of fades away. I want them to know about me though, about us."

Christian wrapped his hand around Eli's, showing that he

Tyler Cook

was still as supportive as he was when they first got together. Like always, he never forced Eli on the subject, but supported him in going his own pace.

Christian's parents could notice the emotional interaction between the two men, and they smiled. Shelly broke the spell that Christian had over Eli by saying, "Well, I'm sure that when you're ready to tell them, they will support you no matter what." She grabbed her husband's hand, which was nearby on top of the table. "We didn't think any different of Christian when he came out to us. And we couldn't be more proud of him and the life that he has made for himself."

Christian's face got red from being in the spotlight. He quickly changed the subject. "So Johnny, caught anything lately?"

The four of them laughed.

***

Because Eli and Christian had arrived at Shelly and Johnny's so late in the evening, they went straight to bed after dinner. Christian had kissed Eli passionately before going off into another room in the house, leaving Eli to himself in the guest room. Eli respected Christian for honoring his traditional values on intimacy. But he couldn't help but desire Christian lying in bed next to him as he slept in an unfamiliar area.

Eli woke up the next morning to someone poking him in the head. He creaked his eyes open enough to see that it was Christian, his face mere inches away from Eli's.

"Wake up, sleepyhead."

Eli was still so groggy, he could barely focus. "How can you be so chipper this early in the morning?"

"Because it's fishing day with Johnny. Don't you want to come with us?"

Being with Christian sounded tempting, but the sleepy state that he was in made him decide against it. "Sleeping in this bed sounds better. Come lay with me."

Christian chuckled. "You're just saying that because you're out of it. You get some more sleep. While we're gone, maybe you and my mom can get to know each other a bit better."

Eli was unsure of that thought. But if it got Christian to leave him alone and let him return to his sleep, he would do it. "Okay, sounds good."

Christian leaned in and kissed him tenderly. "I love you, more than you know."

"I know. But I love you more," Eli said, reversing their statements that they had made on the mountain only days ago.

Christian smiled and rubbed Eli's cheek before exiting the room and closing the door behind him.

Eli couldn't wait to see the love of his life again. Being separated from him already seemed to be a burden that he wasn't able to bear. His only comfort was the black hole of sleep that he didn't hesitate to fall into.

***

When Eli woke up several hours later, the sun was up high in the clouds and pointing directly into the guest bedroom. When his stomach grumbled, he realized that it was lunch time and decided to get up and get ready for the day.

He descended down the stairs a half hour later. When he made it to the bottom of the staircase, he heard sounds and smelt something delicious coming deep within the house. He followed the smell until he reached the glorious kitchen, a part of the house that he didn't get to see the previous night.

"There you are," Shelly said, turning around from the stove to look at Eli. "You must have been exhausted from your trip."

"I was," Eli said. "I usually don't sleep so late, but I couldn't seem to get up today."

"All is well." Shelly turned back around to face the stove and said, "I figured while the boys were out fishing, it would give us a chance to talk."

That made Eli nervous. What did they have to talk about? "Yes, I suppose we can." He sat down at the island counter and waited for the discussion to begin.

"Good," Shelly said, scooping up the food with a spatula and placing it on two plates. She turned around and placed a delicious looking plate in front of him. "I hope you like lamb."

Eli didn't respond. All he could focus on was the food in front of him and started digging in.

"I guess you do," Shelly giggled.

Eli felt ashamed of himself for forgetting his manners. "I'm sorry. I didn't realize how hungry I was."

Shelly patted him on the back as she circled around him and sat next to him. "Don't apologize. When Christian was still with me, he would eat me out of house and home. I'm used to it."

Eli smiled at her and resumed his lunch. He couldn't get over how good of a cook Christian's mother was.

"Eli," Shelly started, "We are so happy to have you with us."

"I'm glad to be here," Eli responded. "You and Johnny have

been so welcoming. To be honest, I was dreading the trip down here."

"Why is that?"

"I don't know," Eli said. He really couldn't form his thoughts to get a clear answer himself. "So many things. Me not being out being one of the major factors."

Shelly nodded. "Christian was the same way when he came down to tell us. He was so nervous; you would have thought that he was ready to confess to murder. But he had no idea how accepting we were. To tell you the truth, a mother knows about these things. I always knew that there was a part of him that he hadn't explored yet. I also knew that it was a matter of time before something would trigger his self-exploration."

"Christian told me that breaking up with his last girlfriend was the cause of that."

"Yes, he told me the same thing," Shelly said. "I'm glad that things ended with her. She was a dreadful thing. Even if it meant pain for him, I knew that it was a step onto the path to happiness."

Eli sat there and continued eating; processing everything that Shelly was telling him.

Shelly continued. "When he brought Jaden with him to introduce him to us, I knew that he was ready to tell us the truth."

"What was he like?" Eli asked, "Jaden, I mean?"

Shelly thought about it for a moment. She held on to her cup of coffee and reminisced in the past. "He was a handsome young man. And he was so comfortable with himself. He came out a lot earlier than Christian did, even though he didn't have his parent's support. He was kind and funny and smart. And he would have gone to Hell and back for Christian, if Christian asked him to."

"Yeah," Eli said with a somber tone. "I have gotten that same impression as well."

The woman set her cup on the counter and put her hand on top of his. "The weekend Christian came down to tell us, he also told us about you, when Jaden wasn't able to hear of course."

Eli was shocked to hear this new discovery. "He did? What did he say?"

"He told us that he had developed feelings for you as well. But it just felt more right with Jaden. He really couldn't explain it to us. It wasn't something that didn't have any logic. It was just a gut feeling. He also told us how he had ended things with you."

Eli nodded his head sadly, having to face what had happened so many years ago.

"I was disappointed with Christian," Shelly said. "Even though he chose Jaden, there was no reason to treat you like that. But he just seemed so happy with Jaden, I somehow overlooked his actions. I hope you will forgive me."

Eli was surprised by Shelly's request. "You don't need to be sorry, Shelly. They loved each other. I've accepted it. True, I was hurt the whole time that I didn't hear from him. But now, I have the understanding and closure that I didn't have before. They were meant to be."

Shelly patted Eli's arm. "It takes a true man to say something like that, even if it meant giving up the person that you love to make them happy."

Eli nodded, but was unsure how she was able to read his thoughts.

"Yes," she said, "I can tell that you love him. And I can also tell that he loves you. You don't have to be a rocket scientist to realize that."

"I do," Eli said, meaning it with all of his heart. "I really do love him."

"And I believe you. I haven't seen him this happy since before—"

Eli knew what she was referring to. "Before Jaden got sick?"

Shelly nodded her head. "It was a shock to us all. Who can make sense of a healthy man like Jaden getting so sick so fast? It destroyed Christian inside; to see the man that he loved fall victim to something so unimaginable. He didn't show it around Jaden, though. He wanted Jaden to be filled with as much positive energy as possible, even though at some point, Christian didn't see how his husband could get better.

"After Jaden passed," Shelly shuddered after saying it, "Christian became a broken shell of his former self. He exiled himself in that house with his cat, and only came out to work. His life died with Jaden, and I thought that all hope for him was lost."

This was nothing that Eli hadn't heard before. But hearing it from Shelly gave a new perspective. He hated to hear this part of Christian's life; how he was lost and alone for so long. But it was who Christian was, and he needed to come to terms with it, just like Christian had.

"But something changed," Shelly resumed, perking up Eli's attention. "One night, he calls me and tells me that he ran into you again."

Eli had never heard this story before. He started paying

243

close attention, haning on to every word that the small woman had to say.

Shelly looked around the room, making sure that there would be no chance that they would be interrupted. "I'm going to tell you something, something that only I and Christian know. And you have to promise me that what I tell you does not leave this room."

"I promise," Eli said, with eagerness in his voice.

Shelly nodded and continued. "You know Christian, always faithful to his significant other. When he first got together with Jaden, he wanted to be completely honest with him. So he told Jaden about you."

Eli could feel a shock wave go through his entire body. This was a new revelation to him. "Jaden knew about me?"

"Yes. Christian told him how he had developed feelings for you before he and Jaden became official. But he made it clear that he chose Jaden, and that he only wanted to be with him. And as proof of that, he would cut all ties from you, even though it wasn't in his nature to do something so cruel to a person."

Eli could barely move, he was so overwhelmed. All of this knowledge and closure that he had desired for so many years, and thought that he had gotten many months ago, started rushing over him.

"Fast forward several years," Shelly said. "Christian was sitting next to Jaden's death bed. The doctor said that it wouldn't be long until he went. We were all there, hoping for a miracle that would never come. Jaden, who was in a bit of pain, told Christian that he needed to tell him something."

Eli was so focused on what she was saying. His eyes were big, and his ears were perked up. He leaned in closer to Shelly. "What did he say?"

Shelly leaned in closer as well. "Jaden said, 'Christian, I love you will all of my heart. I wish I could stay here and grow old with you, but I can't. So I need you to promise me something. Promise me that you'll find Eli. Give him the same love that you've given me. Promise me that you'll be happy with him, and not feel guilty about it. I need you to do this.'"

A big tear escaped Eli's eye duct and splashed on the counter top. He could barely comprehend what he had just been told. Jaden, on the verge of death, using his final moments to make sure that Christian would live on happy. That was true love, Eli thought. And he didn't think that he was even capable of that kind of love.

This must have been what he tried to tell me at Café Stratta, Eli thought.

Shelly wiped a tear from her eyes as well. "As you can tell, Christian didn't follow through his promise, at first. He felt like being happy without Jaden would be a betrayal to his memory. But eventually, I think he understood that Jaden made him make that promise for a reason. He didn't want Christian to be miserable without him, even though he knew that Christian would want to be miserable."

She grabbed Eli's hand with both of hers and held it close to her. "Eli, I'm not a very religious person. But I do know that Christian meeting you at your office was not by chance. I believe that God, or even Jaden played a part in it. You have brought him back to life. And I know that you will love him the way Jaden had hoped."

Eli, face puffy from the tears that were streaming down his face, grabbed Shelly in a big hug. Talking to her meant more to him than anything. Every possible reservation or hesitation that he may have had about Christian was now gone. He also knew that this wasn't just a relationship to help Christian get his mind off of his dead husband. They were meant to be together, just like Christian and Jaden were meant for each other. Eli also believed that Jaden had played a part in all of this; a final gift to the love of his life.

"Thank you," Eli whispered into Shelly's ear.

"No, thank you, Eli," Shelly responded. She pushed Eli back so that she could look into his eyes. "Thank you for giving my son a new reason to live. I know that you'll make him happy. I also know that he will love you with everything that he has."

"I know as well," Eli said, nodding his head.

The two continued to sit there for what seemed like forever, hugging, laughing and crying over their new relationship.

***

"Eli, make sure that Christian comes back down here real soon. And we'll be up to see you as soon as we can."

"Will do," Eli said, hugging Shelly out in the driveway of her home by the sea. He didn't want to leave his new friends, but knew that they couldn't stay forever.

He looked over at Christian, who was talking to Johnny about how they would catch so much more fish the next time they were down there.

Shelly noticed his stare and brought Eli's attention back to her. "Give him everything you've got. I know that it's a decision that you won't regret."

"I will," Eli said, "You have my word."

They hugged one more time as Christian was heading towards the car. Shelly whispered in Eli's ear. "I also know that your parents are so proud of you. They will love you know matter what. Remember that."

Eli looked at her, knowing what she was getting at. Was he capable of telling his family the truth about him and his relationship with Christian? Could he face his darkest fear, which was the chance of rejection by them?

Shelly let him go, allowing him to head to the car. Johnny stopped him, however, right before he had his hand on the door handle. Johnny held his hand out. "Welcome to the family," Johnny said.

Eli shook Johnny's hand, unsure about what he meant. Did he know something that Eli didn't?

He wasn't able to ponder on it much, because Christian honked on the horn and rolled down the window. "Come on, we have to get home before dark."

Eli got inside, ready to return home with his boyfriend.

He waved goodbye to Shelly and Johnny. Shelly ran behind the car, yelling for them to drive safely.

Chapter Twenty-One

Eli thought about his weekend with Christian, Shelly and Johnny the entire way home. Words from Shelly kept ringing in his ears, reminding him that being with Christian was no fluke. He couldn't imagine a life without him, even though he spent years before their relationship wondering if he would ever see the man again.

"Are you okay?" Christian asked, massaging Eli's left shoulder with his free hand, while the other hand kept hold of the steering wheel. "You've been quiet."

Christian's hand on his shoulder felt wonderful. It took every ounce of worry away. He only wished that more of Christian was touching him. "Yeah, I'm fine. Just dreading work tomorrow."

"You and me both."

All of his life, Eli had never let somebody in the way that he had let Christian in. Christian knew so much about Eli's life, there were no longer any details about Eli that Christian didn't know. There were no secrets, nor was there any reason to cause Christian running for the hills. He was there to stay.

***

Christian pulled the car into the driveway of Eli's house and put the car in park. Eli was already missing the company of Christian's parents, but the feeling of being back in his own home was a nice thought too. But he didn't want his time with Christian to end.

Eli grabbed his things from the back of the car and moved

them to the front door of the house. Christian was right behind him, making sure there was help available if Eli needed it.

A sudden urge overcame Eli. It was a feeling that wasn't unfamiliar, but was stronger and potent. Never had he desired a person the way he desired Christian right then and there. Just standing next to him wasn't enough. He wanted the two of them to become one, united in love and passion.

"I guess this is everything," Christian said behind him, leaning forward against the brick wall.

"I guess so." Eli wasn't able to say much else. His mind was filled with thoughts that he had never seriously considered before.

Christian kissed Eli before turning around and started heading towards his blue Nissan truck that he had parked along the edge of the house.

The urge became too much for Eli. He had to have Christian with him tonight. He leaped at Christian and grabbed his arm. Christian turned around as if something was wrong with Eli.

"No, please stay."

"Are you sure?" Christian asked.

"I'm very sure," Eli said. "I don't just want you to stay. I *need* you to stay."

Christian smiled. "Then I'll stay." He turned around to grab his own things to bring inside.

Eli nodded his head, now sure that Christian wasn't going anywhere. "Okay, I'll meet you inside."

He unlocked the door and slipped inside, leaving Christian outside to gather his things.

This is it, Eli thought. *He is the love of your life. It can't get any more special than this.*

Christian made his way inside, with his bags under his arm. "I guess this is everything," he said, setting his things down in the hall way.

Eli stared at Christian, unable to move.

Christian looked concerned. "What is it?"

He did what he felt was right. Eli ran to Christian and kissed him hard on the lips. "I want you. I need you. All of you. Right now."

It took Christian a second to process what Eli was saying. "Are you sure?"

Eli kissed him again. "More sure than I have ever been in my entire life."

They stared at each other again before they came back together in a passionate kiss. Christian's taste was intoxicating to Eli, already feeling drunk off of Christian's love. Christian was tender with his kisses but was now more aggressive, something that Eli had been looking forward to for some time.

Christian made the next move. Eli was glad that Christian was taking the lead, because he didn't want to do something wrong. But he knew that Christian wouldn't care. Christian put his hands on Eli's waist, and slowly moved his way up Eli's body, picking up his shirt as he went. Each movement that Christian made sent shockwaves through Eli's body.

Eli's shirt came over his head, exposing every muscle on the upper part of his body. He had never felt so exposed in his life, but he didn't care. He was in good company.

He placed his lips against Christian's as he did the same

thing to his boyfriend. Touching Christian's skin sent Eli in a wild frenzy. He could feel the waistband of Christian's underwear, then the ripples of Christian's abs. His hands were then on Christian's chest, running through the thin chest hairs as he continued upwards.

Seeing Christian as he was was exactly as Eli had pictured him: beautiful. He felt so lucky to be in the presence of this perfect specimen, and to have that person feel the same way about him.

Eli grabbed hold of Christian and put his lover's hands on his waist, just above the belt loops of his pant. He then did the same to Christian.

"I like a man who takes control," Christian said, joking about how Eli was now leading the intimate encounter.

"Shut up and take my clothes off," Eli growled with passion.

Christian obliged, with Eli matching every action that Christian made. They grabbed a hold of each other's pants and pulled down.

They were now down to their underwear; Eli in his black trunks and Christian in his blue boxers. Eli couldn't stop staring at Christian. It was like looking at a Greek God that was only a myth, a vision of perfection.

"Like what you see?" Christian asked, looking down at himself.

Eli wasn't able to respond. All he could do was kiss the man in front of him, desiring much more than that.

"I'll take that as a yes," Christian responded.

They both smiled. Eli planted his head in the warmth of Christian's chest. Christian then rested his own head on Eli's shoulder.

"This is exactly what I imagined this moment with you would be," Eli said.

Christian kissed Eli's shoulder and slowly moved up his neck and then the side of his face. "What else did you imagine with me?"

Eli entwined his fingers in Christian's and started pulling him down the hall. "I'll show you."

They made their way hastily down the hall, too involved in their own passion to pay any attention to Marik, who was dancing in between them, begging for the love that he thought he deserved.

As they entered the bedroom, Eli turned Christian around, getting a clear view of the man in front of him. He knew that he wanted to do this. This wasn't lust in his heart. It was love. And he knew why Christian was an exception to all of the other people that he had met in the past, and why he was willing to go down a road with Christian that he wasn't ready to go down with anyone else.

All of his life, he had waited to spend this special moment with the right person, and he knew that Christian was that person.

"I love you," Eli said.

"I know. But I love you more."

Eli shut the door behind him and took the remaining article of clothing off of himself. Christian did the same. They were both exposed, but neither noticed their nakedness. They were in their true form: bare down to their soul and beautiful. They kissed passionately, ready to test the limits of their love.

***

It turned out that their love had no limits.

Eli fell on his back in the bed, gasping for breath. He wasn't able to see clearly, his vision compromised by the blurriness and colorful dots that had taken over. He was soaked in sweat from head to toe.

What had just transpired between him and Christian was more than he had expected. He had no idea just how addicting Christian was. And now that their unifying passion had concluded, he craved the man even more, like a drug that he would never be able to quit.

He looked over and saw Christian recovering from the same spell. The man looked absolutely beautiful. There wasn't one aspect of the man that was flawed. Continuing to stare at him caused Eli's addiction to flare up, wanting to start round two.

"Damn, that was amazing," Eli said, rolling over and wrapping himself around Christian. The sweat of each other's bodies were starting to cool, which made the two hot bodies more comfortable.

"You're telling me," Christian said, wiping his brow. "We have to do that again."

Eli was glad that he said that. "That's a promise I expect you to keep, mister."

They laid there for what seemed like hours to Eli. When he was with Christian, time ceased to exist. It was just the two of them. Nothing else matter. All Eli cared about was feeling the rhythm of Christian's breath.

"I want to meet your parents."

Hearing those words from Christian brought Eli back from the sense of euphoria. His crash back to planet Earth was harder for him than he wanted.

Eli lifted his head to look at Christian. "If this is your version of sexy talk, it's not working."

Christian sighed. "Eli, I'm serious. You're the love of my life. And I want—no, I need to know all of the parts of you. Introducing you to my family was a major step for us. And I think we are ready to make that same step with your family."

All Eli could do was stare at Christian, contemplating on what to say. Yes, at one time, he had said that he would come out to his parents, if Christian was in his life. But that was years ago, and that plan never panned out. It felt right and wrong at the same time, pulling him in a million directions.

But looking at Christian, touching Christian, calmed his thoughts. He knew that whatever happened, Christian would be by his side. Even if his family didn't respond well to what he had to tell them. He loved his family with all of his heart, and he knew that they felt the same way about him. But would they think differently once he introduced them to Christian, and exposed his secret that he had been keeping for so many years?

There was only one way to find out.

"Okay."

"You're serious?" Christian asked. He was surprised by how easy the discussion had went.

"Yes, I'm serious," Eli said, laying his head on Christian's chest again. Feeling Christian's hands wrap around him made him feel so much better. He knew that with the love of his life, he would be able to do anything. "I can't hide forever. Nor can I hide you forever. I'm ready to show you off." He kissed Christian on the chest. "But you have to promise me that we will get naked more often."

"Deal," Christian said, pulling the white sheets over their heads to embark on a new adventure of passion.

Chapter Twenty-Two

"I don't know if I can go through with it," Eli said as he got into the passenger seat of Christian's electric car.

"You're going to be fine," Christian said, getting in the opposite seat and turning the car on. "We're going to be fine."

The morning after their night of romance, Eli called his mother and asked if the family wanted to have dinner with him. Diane was thrilled at the thought, complaining that she never got to see her son enough since he moved out. Even though he said that they should come to his house, his mother insisted that she would make dinner.

That shook up Eli's plan, meaning that he was no longer going to be able to do things on his terms. He was going to now have to come out to his family in a setting that was less comfortable to him.

"Can I bring a friend?" Eli asked, barely able to speak up.

"Of course," Diane said. "It'll be nice to meet someone that you spend your free time with."

Is she sure of that?

"Relax," Christian said, deciding to hold Eli's hand. "It's not as bad as you're expecting it to be."

Eli looked over at the man who was driving him to the moment that he had always dreaded. "Speak for yourself. You've been out for years."

"True, but at one time, I had to do the same thing as you. And it was equally painful. But I got through it. And I know that you will too."

Eli wasn't so sure of that. He had spent years playing the scenario in his head, imagining the moment when he told his parents and his siblings the truth about his sexuality. Every time he thought of it, the end result turned grim; images of his family heartbroken and disappointed at him for the decision that he had made for his life.

Except that he didn't make this decision. He had no more control over his sexuality than he did with his feelings towards Christian. It was something that was there, and it was something that everyone would eventually have to live with.

"So, who will be at dinner tonight?" Christian asked, bringing Eli out of his internal debate on whether or not to back out of this crazy idea.

"Well there are my parents, of course. Then there's my sister, Ruth. She is in her last year of high school. And then there's Carrie, who is a senior at the community college. She's bringing her boyfriend, Landon, who I've never met before."

"See," Christian said, looking on the bright side, "You won't be the only one that is feeling awkward at this dinner."

Eli decided to be sarcastic. "You're right. Maybe Carrie will announce that she's pregnant tonight."

***

Christian pulled into the driveway of Eli's old home. Even though he visited his family often, the house felt like a distant memory to Eli. He was afraid that he had distanced himself from his family to be more himself. That was all about to change, though.

Christian pulled the car into park. He couldn't help but

stare at the large house. "This house is beautiful."

"Not like your parent's castle by the sea," Eli responded. He didn't intend for it to sound as rude as it seemed.

Christian put his hand on Eli's cheek. "Are you ready? I know that you're going to do great. If there is anyone that I know that can conquer their fears, it's you. Just know that no matter what happens, I love you. And I'll always be here for you."

Eli knew what Christian said was true. No matter how angry and disappointed his family would be for telling them the truth, he knew that he could always rely on the man beside him; the man that he loved.

"I guess I'm as ready as I'll ever be."

The two men got out of the car and started walking towards the front door. As they made their way, Christian walked up beside Eli and put his hand in Eli's. Eli knew that he would not have been able to do this without the man beside him. He owed what little courage that he had to Christian. He hoped Christian loved him just as much as he said that he did. Because there was a chance that he would be the only one left in Eli's life after this dinner.

They broke their connection, letting go of each other's hands as Eli rang the bell. They stood there, waiting for whatever lied ahead of them.

Eli's sister, Ruth, was the one to open the door. "About time that you got here. We were starting to think that you weren't coming."

Eli ruffled his sister's hair as he started to walk inside the house. Eli looked over at Christian as he said, "There is nowhere else I would rather be right now."

Immediately to their left was the dining room lit up and the table filled with food. Everyone was there, except Diane, including a new male face that Eli had never seen before. He assumed that it was Carrie's new beau, Landon.

"Hi everybody," Eli said, waving as he walked closer into the room. He noticed that Christian was keeping a safe distance away.

"Hi, son," his father said, waving them closer into the room. He got up and held his hand out for Christian. "Hi, I'm Eli's father, Charlie."

"Nice to meet you," Christian said, grabbing Charlie's hand in a firm handshake. "I'm Christian."

"Is my baby here?" Asked a distant voice deeper into the house.

"Yes, honey," Charlie yelled back so she could hear. "Hurry on out before the food gets even colder."

Diane quickly appeared at the opposite end of the room, with a basket full of rolls in her hands. "I'm here, I'm sorry." When her eyes found Eli, she set the basket down on the table and held her hands out for a hug from her son. "I'm so glad that you came, Eli."

"Me too," Eli lied. He wanted nothing more than to be somewhere else, somewhere that he could hide from the truth, which was the easiest thing to do over the years.

Once his mother broke their embrace, Diane eyed Christian and smiled. "Hi, I'm Eli's mother."

Christian held out his hand to shake Eli's mother's hand. "I'm Christian. I'm Eli's —"

"Boyfriend," Eli blurted out.

Everybody's jaws dropped, including Christian's. Even he was surprised by the spontaneous way that Eli came out.

Eli couldn't believe it. He just came out. There was no rhyme or reason to why he did it. It was an instant decision that Eli made, using Christian's introduction to rip the very painful band-aid off. He couldn't feel anything, but he was waiting for the metaphorical blood to start pouring out of his soul.

Everybody was broken out of the awkward trance that Eli had put them in once Landon leaned over next to Carrie and said, "You didn't tell me that your brother was gay."

Diane made an awkward laugh before she shook Christian's hand. "Hello Christian, it's a pleasure meeting Eli's...boyfriend."

The awkwardness was starting to kill Eli inside. He had to do something to start damage control. "I'm sorry that I dropped this huge bomb on all of you. This is why I wanted to have dinner with you all. And I figured instead of stewing in it any longer, I would just go ahead and tell you all."

Diane remained silent and motioned the two men to the table. "Please, let's sit down and eat before the food gets cold."

Eli and Christian sat down at the two empty seats. Once they were seated, Christian put his hand on Eli's knee to try and show his support. This was certainly not how Eli had wanted things to go. And now, he couldn't get a read on how his family was reacting to the news.

"Are you disappointed in me?" Eli braced for the worst outcome to occur, making his worst fears a reality.

Diane and Charlie reached out and grabbed each other's

hand. "Honey," Diane said with a weak smile on her face, "Your father and I always thought that you were attracted to men on some level. We're just shocked that you chose this dinner to do it. I guess it's just a surprise to have our suspicions confirmed and to find out that you have a boyfriend all at once."

Eli just sat there, trying to take it all in.

"Your mother and I are proud of you, no matter what," Charlie spoke up. "You have made a great life for yourself, and we are glad that you have *finally* found someone to share your life with." Eli's parents looked at each other for a moment before Charlie said, "We thought for years that you were going to be alone and be celibate for the rest of your life."

Everybody started laughing. Even Eli couldn't help but chuckled a bit. Christian reached out for Eli's nearby hand. Eli looked towards his boyfriend, and it was as if they could read each other's mind. Christian's eye contact told him that he believed that there wasn't ever anything to be afraid of.

Knowing the truth about how his parents felt caused a wave of relief to overcome Eli's body. Had he known that his parents had suspected his sexuality for years, he would have told them. He knew that every newly ousted man felt the same way. Hindsight was always twenty-twenty.

"Did you know?" Eli asked his sisters. He was curious if his sisters had had the same suspicions. The family finally started passing food around to put on their plates.

"I knew," Ruth spoke up, keeping her eyes glued to her cell phone that was in her hands. "When your brother never mentions being in a relationship, or even having a crush with someone, you can't help but believe that there was something that he wasn't telling you."

Eli knew that Ruth was an observant person. He should have known that she would have seen right through him.

Eli then looked at Carrie. "And you?"

Carrie shrugged her shoulders. "I never really paid any attention to your love life, or—"

"Anything that didn't concern you?" Eli joked. Christian poked Eli to stop his insults as Eli's parents shushed him. Eli looked at his sister with an apologetic look on his face. "I'm sorry, Carrie, I was just kidding."

Carrie shrugged again. "I would be offended if it wasn't true."

Everybody laughed again, including Landon, who had sat there and watched his girlfriend get insulted.

He won't last, Eli thought to himself.

Landon did decided to enter into the conversation. "So how long have you liked dudes?"

It was clear that Carrie's boyfriend wasn't comfortable with the fact of Eli and Christian being romantically linked. The man asked the question like a child would ask why the sky was blue.

Eli wanted to set the record straight, not just towards Landon, but to his whole family. "Well actually, I'm attracted to both genders. But I guess I've always known."

Landon didn't counter back with another question. He resumed to acting oblivious, just like Eli's sister.

"So Eli," his mother started, bringing the attention back towards him. "How long have you and Christian been dating?"

Eli looked at Christian to get help on how long they had been together. But he already knew the answer. How could he forget how long he had been with the best man on Earth? "Seven months."

That sent a shock wave through his mother's face. Diane looked to Charlie for support, who was equally shocked. "Seven months? And you're just now telling us about this?"

The way his mother said it made Eli question whether they were wondering why it took him so long to tell them about Christian, or why Eli had been with a man for that long. Eli then became less optimistic of his family's support. "Well, I wasn't sure how you would react to all of this. Not that I didn't want to show Christian off to you. I knew you would all like him. I just didn't think that you would support my decision to be with him."

Diane then looked upset. This was turning out to be exactly what Eli had feared. "So is this why you have been like a stranger to us for seven plus months? Because you didn't want to tell us the truth about your life? Did you think that we wouldn't accept you?"

Eli's palms started to get sweaty. He didn't want to be here anymore. He just wanted to grab Christian and run out the front door while they had a chance. But he knew that was no longer an option. "Well, I don't know, to be honest. It seemed like you all could go either way. And it just felt easier to be myself when I didn't have this worry of whether you would judge me over my head."

A tear began to form and started to fall down Diane's cheek. Seeing her like this made Eli's heart break. It was exactly as he feared.

"I see," she said, placing the cloth napkin to the side of her plate and getting up from seat. "Please excuse me." She started to walk away from the table and towards the master bedroom before she turned around and looked at Christian. "It was a pleasure to meet you, Christian."

"Same to you, Mrs. Cooper," Christian said as she continued walking away.

Eli sat there, unable to move, feeling his heart break piece by piece. The rest of the family sat there, silent from the upsetting encounter. Were they feeling the same way about him inside? Without his family, how was he supposed to live his life happily?

"Go talk to her," Christian said, nudging Eli in the master bedroom's direction.

He didn't want to, afraid that more sadness would overcome him and his family. But Eli knew that he had to do it. He needed to do as much as he could to maintain his relationship with his mother, and hold his family together. At least he could say that he tried if things didn't work out.

He got up and walked to his parent's bedroom. It had been so long since he had been in this house. Would it also be the last time?

He knocked on the door and heard a soft "Come in" come from inside the room. He opened the door and entered, seeing his mother sob, her black mascara smudged and running down her face.

"Oh, mom," he said, deciding to sit on the edge of the bed. "I didn't want this to upset you. I feared that it would, which was why I didn't want to tell you anything. I know you're disappointed in me, and you don't wish this lifestyle on me. But it's who I am.

And I love Christian, just as much as I love you and the rest of the brood. I hope you can understand and accept me for who I am, because I can't bear to lose you. I need you."

By that time, tears were streaming down his face. He told himself that he needed to be strong, but he couldn't help but feel like the child that he had been so many years ago, desperate for his mother who was there for him when something was wrong in his life. He didn't know what he would do without her.

His mother then stopped crying, realizing that her son was now crying. She reached her hand out to touch his. "Oh honey, I…I'm not judging you for who you are. There is nothing that you could do that would stop me from being proud of you."

That didn't make sense to Eli. "Then what's the matter?"

"The fact that you have been dating this amazing man, and you haven't told your father or I. Or the fact that you have been dealing with this inner struggle for all of your life, and the reason is because you thought that we wouldn't accept you. And then you limit your visits and communication with us because it is easier to be yourself without us."

Things were starting to make sense for him now. She was upset because he hadn't told her all of these things, instead of telling them tonight. "If I had known that you would have been okay with it, I would have told you years ago. I just never got a read on how you felt about this sort of stuff."

Diane nodded her head. "I guess that's our fault."

"Why do you say that?"

"Because," Diane said, letting her head rest on the nearby pillow, "Your father and I had discussed multiple times over the years to confront you about it. I know that sounds bad, like we wanted to ambush you or something. But that wasn't the case. We just wanted to talk to you about it, let you know that you had our support."

Hearing that shocked Eli. All of his life, his parents had supported him, and even knew that he had sexual feelings towards men. And all of this time, he had been keeping his secret, fearing that if his parents found out, they would disown him.

"We decided against it though," Eli's mother said. "We thought that we shouldn't take the choice of telling us away from you. We knew that when you felt ready, you would tell us."

Knowing this made Eli feel good. Knowing that they wanted to respect his privacy made him feel more loved than possible. With Christian and Eli's family, he could truly be happy.

"I wish you would have confronted me, though," Eli said. "It would have forced me to face my fears and be myself. I know that you wanted to respect my privacy, but knowing that you would have supported me, no matter what, would have meant more to me."

"I know. I guess we are both at fault here."

Eli reached out and embraced his mother in a hug. "You don't have to worry, mama. There is nothing that could take me away from you. And I'm never going to leave you."

"I believe you, baby," his mother said, patting him on the back.

They were both wiping their eyes when Eli said, "Let's dry up our tears and go back out there. I want you to really meet Christian, now that all of this awkwardness is over with."

Eli started heading for the door when his mother said "Wait."

He turned around, watching his mother pat on the bed, indicating that they weren't done talking. He walked back towards the bed and sat next to his mother.

"I wanted to ask about Christian. Do you really have feelings for him?"

Eli nodded proudly. This was a question that he could answer without hesitation. "I do. He's *the one*. That, I have no doubt."

That made his mother smile. "Good. I'm glad that you have found someone that makes you happy. That is all I have ever hoped for you."

Eli's heart was starting to overflow with joy. He hugged his mother, increasing his grip on her. "I love you, mom."

"I love you too, baby. You have to promise me that you'll bring Christian over more so we all can get a chance to know him better."

"That's a deal."

His mother pushed him away, got up and walked towards the door. "Come on, we don't want to keep everyone waiting."

Eli didn't waste any time. He couldn't wait to get back out there, with both his family and his boyfriend, enjoying his new outlook on life.

***

Besides the tension at the beginning of dinner, the night with Eli's family went rather well. He spent the evening catching up with his family and informing them on all of the new things that had occurred in his life. Then he sat and listened to his family talking to Christian, asking him questions in an attempt to get to know him better. Eli had no doubt that they liked him. Christian made them laugh several times, and even Christian and Charlie got on the topic of computer repair. Eli tuned out of the conversation as the older Zane finally came into the dining room, jumped on Eli's lap and took a nap as he was petted.

Towards the end of the night, it was just Eli, Christian and Eli's parents left, sitting in the living room and chatting about nothing in particular. Ruth had decided to go to bed and get ready for school, while Carrie went off with Landon to do God knows what.

Eli looked at his watch and saw that it was well past midnight. "Wow, we better head home. I've got work early in the morning, and Christian still needs to get home after I take him back to his car."

They all got up from their comfortable positions and started heading towards the front door.

While Charlie and Christian were off to the side shaking hands and talking more about their technology interests, Eli's mother embraced him in a hug one more time. She put her mouth close to his ears before speaking in a whisper.

"He's perfect, Eli. I'm so glad that you have found someone that can make you happy."

Hearing her approval of Christian made Eli's heart warm up. "Thank you. I can't tell you how good it feels to be completely honest with you now."

"Me too." She waited a moment for Christian and Charlie to reach a break in their conversation before she spoke up. "I expect you two to visit us more often now that the awkward coming out party has ended."

Eli laughed awkwardly. He still couldn't believe that he was out to his parents. It was even weirder to believe that they supported him fully, and even liked his boyfriend. His future seemed brighter than ever, and he couldn't wait to resume his relationship with the family that he treasured so dearly.

"Yes ma'am," Christian said, wrapping his arm around Eli's waist. "I'll never say no to your good cooking."

Diane waved off the compliment and kissed Eli lightly on the cheek. "Love ya, baby."

"I love you too."

Eli barely broke away from his mother before he was embraced by his father. "I'm proud of you, son," Charlie said.

They all continued to say goodbye and shake hands before Eli and Christian finally made it outside, and Eli's parents had closed the door behind them.

Eli felt weird inside. It was as if he was stepping out into his new life; a life where his love and his parents could co-exist. It was something that he had only dreamed about. He never thought that it would become a reality, nor something that his parents would be proud of.

His thinking was cut off once Christian reached out and put his hand in Eli's. "You see? I told you that everything was going to be fine."

"I just can't believe it," Eli said, making his way down the stairs with Christian leading the way. "I knew that either they would freak out, or they would accept it. I had no idea with how supportive they all would be."

Christian held the passenger door open for Eli as they made it to his car. "You know, sometimes you have to let the truth out. Tonight, you not only became honest with yourself and your family, but you also repaired a deteriorating relationship with your family that nobody knew was occurring."

He shut the door before Eli could respond. He was right. If Eli hadn't had told them tonight, who knew how long he would have waited to tell them. And the longer he had waited, the further distant he would have become with the family that he cared so much for. He couldn't help but feel guilty, though, for making his mother cry tonight. It hadn't had dawned on him that his secret had put a toll on them too.

On the way home, Christian couldn't help but talk about how nice Eli's parents were. He talked about how good the food Diane prepared was, then he talked about all of the interests that he and Charlie had together.

Eli was pleased that Christian had found his way into Eli's family, but he wasn't paying any attention to his boyfriend as he talked. He couldn't stop repeating the night's events in his head, trying to find some reason to believe that all that had happened was a dream, or a fake reaction that his parents had put up to make him not feel so bad about himself.

"I did the same thing, you know."

Eli didn't understand what Christian was saying. "I'm sorry?"

"You're questioning everything that happened tonight. You're wondering if your parents were genuine with their support, and if they really are okay with me."

It was as if the man could read him like a book. "How did

you know that?"

Christian smiled. "Because I went through the same thing when I came out. I believed that the only reason that my parents didn't blow up was because Jaden was there to witness to my possible murder. But very quickly, I found out that they really didn't think of me any differently."

It made Eli feel good to know that he wasn't the only one that had felt this way before, nor would he be the last. "I spent my whole life questioning my feelings and wondering how my family would act if and when I told them the truth. I don't know how my life will be from this moment forward."

"You'll finally get to live your life," Christian replied. "And better than that, you'll get to live it with me."

Eli hoped that that was a promise that Christian planned on keeping forever.

They had returned back to Eli's house, Marik eagerly waiting for them to let him into the house. They walked to the front door, holding hands.

"Thank you so much for being there for me," Eli said as he started to unlock the door. "I couldn't have done it without you."

"Yes, you could have," Christian countered back. "You're stronger than you give yourself credit. But I was happy to be there for you and lend you any support that you needed."

A sudden rush of passion overcame Eli as he stood in the house, with Christian one step down outside, and Marik hurriedly running by them to get inside. Eli grabbed Christian by the shirt and pulled him closer for a kiss.

"Now let me be here for you," Eli said, pulling Christian

inside and taking off his shirt for him.

Christian didn't question it. He took of Eli's shirt and pushed him towards the bedroom, shutting the front door behind them.

Chapter Twenty-Three

Several months had passed since Eli had worked up the courage to come out to his family. And since then, he felt free.

During that time, Eli and Christian had made time to visit their parents. They would go out to eat, or take weekend trips to the coast. Eli enjoyed getting to know Christian's parent's better, and Christian's mother was thrilled to know that he had made the important step for the rest of his life. Christian had also made it clear how much he enjoyed being with Eli's parents, while Charlie and Diane had made the same comments about Christian.

Also since coming out, Eli was no longer afraid to show Christian off to the rest of the world. He started slowly introducing Christian as his boyfriend to the rest of the office. Before he knew it, the whole office knew, and there weren't any whispers of discomfort among them. He felt like the first time in his life, he could be himself.

Today was a cold day in Pinecrest. The snow was slightly blowing through the trees on top of the mountains. From his office, Eli could see the large wall of snow beyond the mountain tops. It wouldn't make it over, but the thought that it could caused excitement within Eli. He loved the snow, but he hated the cold weather. They said that spring was due at anytime, but Eli didn't believe it.

"Eli, you have a call on line one," Caroline said on the intercom.

He rushed over to the phone on his desk and pressed the button that was flashing red. "This is Eli. "

"Hey, babe," said Christian.

Eli couldn't help but smile when Christian acted slightly immature. "What's up?"

It was a moment before Christian spoke. "I was thinking that we could go out tonight and get a warm meal. What do ya think?"

He didn't have to ask Eli twice. "That sounds great," Eli replied, looking outside the window, where the snow was finally starting to come down harder.

"Okay, I'll pick you up. Wear something nice."

Eli wasn't sure whether Christian was planning on taking him somewhere ritzy, or if the man was joking about his wardrobe. Either way, he promised he would and hung up the phone, glad that he had something to look forward to at the end of the day.

***

Later that day, Eli spent a long time getting ready. He broke out the fancy clothing, something that he hated to do. By the time that he was finished, he was dressed in a tucked-in, white button-up shirt, a silver vest, and a skinny, black tie. Either Christian was going to love it, or he was going to laugh his head off because Eli took him so seriously.

I guess I'll find out soon enough.

It wasn't long afterwards that Christian was pulling into the driveway. Once he got out of the car, Eli noticed that Christian was dressed in similar clothing. He had been serious after all.

Eli locked the door behind him before stepping outside. "You weren't kidding about dressing up tonight, were you?"

Christian shook his head, smiling. "Of course not. Why

would I joke about wanting to see you look absolutely amazing?"

Eli's lips were against Christian's before Eli had a chance to give his answer. By the time they broke apart, Eli couldn't remember what the question was.

"So what's the special occasion?" Eli asked.

After they both got in the car, Christian said, "I just felt like we both deserved to go somewhere fancy."

That didn't seem like something out of the box. "Okay. So where are we going?"

"You'll see."

As they made their way down the road, Christian decided to turn the knob on the car's volume control, his hand shaking as he did it. Eli noticed it and wondered what could be wrong with the man.

"Are you okay?"

Once Christian realized what Eli was asking about, he put his hand back on the wheel. "Yeah, I just didn't eat at all today."

Eli hoped he hadn't starved himself so they could go to this dinner. "I guess it's a good thing that we are going for a good meal then."

He had no idea where Christian was driving them, so he didn't pay much attention to when they started driving by the walkway. But questions began popping in his head once Christian turned on his signal light to indicate that he was turning.

"Why are we coming here?"

Christian was speechless for a moment before he said, "I…I think the tire is low. I wanna check it out before we drive any further."

Eli didn't feel the car being lopsided. But he supposed that

Christian would feel it more than Eli, since he was the one driving.

Once they were parked, Christian got out and went towards the end of the car, and out of Eli's sight. The cold air, and a couple of snow flurries, rushed into the car, giving Eli goose bumps all over his arms. He had wished that Christian had shut the door before he left.

"Hey, Eli, can you come back here and help me, please?"

Eli was happy to help, if that meant that they would be back in the warm car, and back on their way to the restaurant. He unbuckled his seatbelt and got out of the car.

It was even colder outside of the car. He regretted getting out as soon as he set foot on the pavement. Larger snowflakes began falling from the sky.

Maybe it'll make it over the mountain after all.

"Did you find the problem?" Eli asked as he walked towards the back of the car.

What he found shocked him to no end.

In front of him was Christian, kneeling down on one knee, waiting for Eli to make his way to the middle of the parking lot.

Eli couldn't believe it. No, Christian wasn't doing what he thought he was doing.

"Are you hurt?" Eli asked, edging closer to his boyfriend.

Christian laughed slightly. "No, Eli, I'm not hurt."

"Then what are you doing?" Eli questioned, already knowing what the answer was.

"I have to ask you a question," Christian responded.

Oh. My. God.

He said his thoughts out loud as well before Christian began speaking.

"Eli, five years ago, here, in this parking lot, I turned my back on you. And even though I had strong feelings for you, I put my feelings aside to be with someone that I also truly loved."

Eli could barely breathe. Tears were starting to swell in his eyes. All of his life, he had hoped for this moment. But he never thought that it would. And now it was. With Christian.

"When Jaden died, I didn't think I could live again, let alone love again. You proved me wrong on both counts. I love you so much, and I can't even imagine a world without you. You're *the one*, Eli, and I don't want to spend another minute without you."

Christian then reached inside his pocket and pulled out a black ring box. Eli could barely breath, he was in such surprise. That, and the cold that was cutting off the circulation from the rest of his body. He could barely gasp for breath when Christian pulled the box open. Inside was a white gold band with a brushed finish. It was simple and classic, just like his love for Christian.

He looked at the ring further. He had always thought that engagement rings were just another stereotype for two men in a relationship. But he couldn't help but admire how beautiful it was. Every aspect of this proposal was meticulously planned. There was no telling how long Christian had been planning this.

"Eli," Christian resumed, gasping for air as well from the cold air, "I let you go five years ago, but I'm not going to let that happen again. We have grown so much with each other, and I want to grow old with you. I'm like your grandparents. If you're not in my life, I won't be able to live. I left you here, I got together with you here, and I want to start the rest of my life with you here.

I hope you will do the honor of marrying me."

Eli didn't even have to think about it for long. "Did you even have to ask? Of course I will."

Eli rushed to Christian as Christian got up from his kneeling position, embracing each other in a powerful kiss. When they were done, they stood there, locked together in a hug.

"I love you so much," Christian whispered in Eli's ear. "More than you can imagine."

"I know," Eli said, smiling. "But I love you more."

Christian smiled, breaking away from his new fiancé in order to put the newly purchased engagement ring on Eli's finger. "You're mine. Forever."

"And ever and ever."

Christian kissed Eli one more time before saying, "We better go and celebrate, before we are late meeting the rest."

"The rest?" Eli asked, "Who all is meeting us?"

"Just all of my family and all of yours."

Eli opened the door to the passenger side of the car, ready to get back in and get warm. "You must have been confident that I would say yes."

"You know me, always the romantic," Christian said, winking.

They pulled out of the parking lot, ready to meet up with their families to celebrate, and start the journey of their lives together.

Epilogue

Two Years Later

"Eli!" Christian yelled from across the house. "Where is the screwdriver?"

He honestly had no idea. "Under the sink...I guess," Eli responded.

After a few minutes had passed, Christian returned to the room that Eli was in. He knelt down next to the many wooden pieces in front of him, and picked a piece up. "It's a good thing that I remembered where I put my tool bag. If it wasn't for me, we wouldn't have a screwdriver to put this cradle together."

"Shut up and hold this thing up," Eli said, smirking as he said it.

"You're the boss, honey."

It had been a year and a half since their wedding day. And not a day had gone by that Eli wasn't happy with the person that he chose to spend the rest of his life with. Christian decided to sell his house on the hill, and the acres of mountain land that was behind it. He felt like it was time to finally bury that part of his past, and let it rest in peace. They decided to stay in Eli's grandparent's home; keeping the love and happiness flowing through the walls that had stood for decades.

But even though Eli and Christian couldn't be happier, there was one thing that they felt was missing from their lives; a child.

"I don't know why we had to run out and buy a cradle," Christian said, starting to screw in some bolts into a piece of the baby bed. "Tori only told us a couple of weeks ago that the in vitro worked."

It had made Eli so sad when Tori came to him and said that the engagement to Chris had come to an end. She said that the breakup was mutual, but Eli didn't believe her. He didn't push her though, because he knew that everyone needed to deal with their own secrets, and find the time to face them. Eli knew that she would make it through, just like he had.

Eli was shocked when she then came to him and offered to carry his and Christian's baby. They had been looking into finding a surrogate, and they had asked Tori for any potential candidates that she thought would be suitable.

"What about me?" she asked.

Eli wasn't so sure about the idea. "I love you, Tori, but you have just ended things with Chris. I feel like you need to find yourself again. Doing this surrogacy would be a lot of responsibility on you."

Tori shook her head with understanding. "I know, but I want—no, I need to do it. How rewarding would it be to be able to birth my best friend's baby? I love you like the brother I never had, and I want to be here for you, like you have always been there for me. You and Christian deserve to be parents, so if I'm able to make that happen, I'm going to do it."

Eli knew that she was going to be okay. And he couldn't wait to spend more time with her, and his future child.

"Ow!" Christian yelped, dropping the screwdriver and wood to the ground and sucking on his finger. "That's it, I give up!"

Eli tried not to laugh, rising to sit in the rocking chair that they had also purchased to put in the future nursery. "That's okay. Take a break. We have several months to get things ready."

Christian didn't resist getting out of the current task and got up and leaned against the rocking chair that Eli was sitting in. "I think it'll have your eyes."

"You think so?"

Eli still couldn't understand why Christian insisted on him being the birth father of the baby. He kept asking Christian why he wanted Eli to be the biological father, and all Christian would say was, "I want little versions of you running around the house." Eli promised Christian that the first-born would be his if the next one would be Christian's. Eli didn't get much resistance.

"I know so," Christian answered. "And I know that I'll love the little thing just about as much, if not more than you."

"I guess the kid'll need to get used to not being out of your sight then." That comment from Eli made the both of them laugh.

Christian kneeled down next to Eli, looking deeply into Eli's eyes. Even after the past two years, Eli was still unable to look away from Christian whenever he gave him that look. It was as if the man was putting him in a trance, making Eli putty at his command.

"What?" Eli asked, rubbing his hands through Christian's hair.

"I'm just thinking how lucky I am to be married to you."

Eli shook his head with disagreement. "No, I think I'm the lucky one."

"No matter how this baby will change our lives, I'm going to give it my all," Christian said. "All of this is going to be worth it, because in the end, I will be able to grow old with you and watch the accomplishments we make together. With you by my side, I'm ready to encounter anything."

Eli couldn't help but let the breath exhale out of his body, like he was a big balloon that was deflating. Every time Christian said things like that, he would melt like hot butter. Eli felt the same way about Christian, and was glad that he had found the love of his life to encounter the big adventure that life had to offer them. Christian was *the one*, and there would never be another person on this earth that would be able to steal Eli's heart the way Christian had.

"Here's to forever," Eli said.

"To forever."

Thank you to all who have read this book. For clarification, no person, buisness or organization paid to be featured in this book. If they were mentioned, it was because I felt it appropriate to include them in the book.

Enjoyed what you read?

Make sure to continue your support for Tyler Cook by following him via his social media accounts:

www.tylermcook.com

www.facebook.com/tylercookbooks

www.twitter.com/tylercook4

www.instagram.com/tylercook4

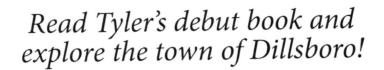
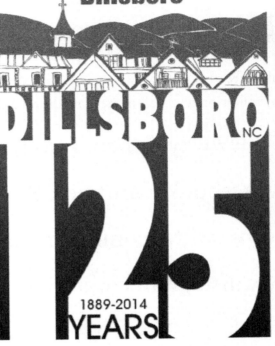

CPSIA information can be obtained
at www.ICGtesting.com
Printed in the USA
LVOW04s1736171116

513427LV00010B/868/P